CONTENTS

SYNOPSIS

Fake dating my high school crush, what could possibly go wrong?

Music is my life, my band is my heart and soul, and it's all falling apart before my eyes.

Paris is a gay icon, my best friend's twin brother, and the crush I never quite got over. And as we both watch our careers burn down around us, we hatch a desperate plan to stay relevant. And if we have a little fun along the way, where's the harm in that?

The band is spiraling, his football career is going up in flames, and the more the world falls down around us, the easier it is to get lost in each other.

But are stolen moments during our own busy schedules and hurried kisses hidden behind social media posts the basis for a real relationship, or is this just another thing that's going to turn to dust in our hands?

**Strike a Chord is the fourth and final book in the Replay series. This series can be read in any order.

COPYRIGHT

cover design by Natasha Snow

Editing by Rebecca J Cartee

MESSAGE FROM THE AUTHOR

With this being the final book in the Replay Series, I just want to take a second to say a huge thank you for reading and falling in love with these beautifully damaged men as much as I did. When the first chapter of Face the Music popped into my head over a year ago, completely unexpectedly, I cried through writing it and couldn't stop thinking about it for days afterward. I was still in the middle of my Heathens Ink series, but Lincoln refused to let me focus on anyone but him. He was tired of waiting to reconcile with his long-lost love, Jace, and the more I got to know the two of them, the more desperate I became for their story as well. This series made my heart bleed and my soul sing in so many different ways. I fell so in love with Lincoln, Lando, Jude, and Benji and it was extremely difficult typing The End on Downward Spiral. I'm hoping to write a spin-off (or a few ��) and hopefully the guys will pop back up along the way. Thank you again for following me on this journey and for reading and enjoying all my books.

Love,
K.M.Neuhold

TRACK 1: SIDE A

Whoever You Want Me To Be

Benji

The strong bassline pounds in my chest, the music becoming a heartbeat all its own as it courses through me. Bodies move around me like an unruly ocean, and I'm lost at sea. Sometimes I hate this feeling, disappearing into the crowd, being nameless and faceless in the dark, pulsing lights of the club. Other times, I crave it like oxygen. For a few brief seconds I'm not a member of the biggest rock band on the planet. I'm not the guy whose face is plastered on magazines and posters and t-shirts. I'm not the person who lays awake at night waiting for the phone call that one of my best friends is dead by their own reckless hand.

I lick my dry lips and lift my drink to them, savoring the burning taste of alcohol on my tongue as I throw the shot back.

"Benji!" A familiar voice breaks through the loud drone of club noise. I glance over my shoulder to find Cooper pushing his way through the crowd. He gets surprised and excited looks from people as he shoves them out of the way. *Yes, you just got elbowed by a rock star*.

"Coop," I greet him, holding my fist up for a bump when he reaches me.

"What are you doing down here? Come up to VIP," he says, grabbing my arm and tugging me without waiting for my response.

We get even more wide-eyed looks as he drags me through the horde of bodies toward the stairs that lead to the VIP level. People take in my long blond hair, pulled into a messy bun on the top of my head, the tattoos covering my arms, and they realize who I am, but not soon enough to get a piece of me before I'm whisked away.

Ten years and most days it still feels like a dream. If I could go back in time and tell the nerdy thirteen-year-old hiding in the janitor's closet to keep from getting the shit kicked out of him that one day he'd be a millionaire, playing keyboard for a chart-topping band, he wouldn't believe it.

The way things are going, it won't be true for long. Thoughts of what's happening to the band are what drove me out of my quiet apartment tonight, dead set on finding as many distractions as possible. Even if Jude manages to not snort his way to an early grave and Lincoln doesn't "accidentally" cut himself too deep again and bleed out, we still have the little problem of Lando being unable to write music anymore. It's starting to feel like one way or another, Downward Spiral isn't going to make it into the new year, which is only a few weeks away.

We reach the VIP lounge and I'm met with a sight my thirteen-year-old self *definitely* wouldn't have believed—actors, models, generally rich and beautiful people are draped over every surface, stroking each other's egos and sipping from twenty-thousand-dollar bottles of champagne like it's water.

Dax James, host of a recently popular reality dating show, catches my eye and looks like he's about to faint.

"Holy shit, you're Benji Casparian," he gasps, his cheeks tingeing pink when he realizes he's broken the cardinal rule of the VIP section—act unimpressed, pretend you belong.

I give him a friendly smile, warmth and pride surging through me. *I am someone.*

"Hey, it's Dax, right?" I offer my hand to shake while Cooper skirts around me to return to what I assume was his spot, in the center of a crowd of other celebrities. I look at how quickly he's accepted into the group and try to reassure myself that even if Downward Spiral breaks up, that doesn't mean I have to give all of this up. Cooper's band, Last Weekend, has been *on a break* for nearly two years, and he doesn't seem to be fazed by it. Of course, it doesn't hurt that he's gone out of his way to stay in the spotlight in the meantime—doing celebrity dating shows, guest hosting a season of some make-me-a-star singing show, you name it.

"Oh my god, I can't believe you know who I am," Dax says, his smile turning flirty as he reaches out and puts a hand on my forearm.

I consider the unspoken offer for several seconds. In the back of my mind, it's become second nature to weigh the possible tabloid or media exposure I could get if I'm caught with whoever's trying to take me to bed. Dax is hot right now, and he's also cute as hell. I'm sure we could have a good time. I glance up and see another man; he looks slightly familiar too... I think he might be the cameraman slash co-host of Dax's show...Milo or something? And he's looking at Dax's hand on my arm like he wants to march over here and tear my arm right off for daring to be touched by Dax.

"It was really nice to meet you. I need to grab a drink and have a chat with my friend Cooper, but you have a good night, okay?"

Dax's face falls a little as he pulls his hand back and nods in understanding. "It was nice to meet you too."

I make my way into the crowd surrounding Cooper, and when he spots me, he smiles brightly again.

"Dude, hold my drink for me real quick," he asks, shoving the half-empty bottle of tequila in my direction.

I take it and help myself to a quick taste. It goes down smooth like expensive liquor should. It doesn't occur to me to ask why I'm holding it for him until everyone starts to back up a little.

"What—" Before I can get the question out, Cooper is getting up on the nearest table.

"Don't try this at home, kids," he advises with a wink. Then, he does a backflip off the table, eliciting cheers and applause from the small crowd.

I laugh and shake my head, taking another drink from the bottle of tequila and then handing it back to him when he holds his hand out for it. He's glowing under the attention, and when he flings his arm over my shoulders, the coveted sense of validation lights me up as well.

I feel my phone vibrate in my pocket, and my heart skips a beat like it always does now. The fear of what might be waiting for me when I answer is an ever-present demon in my life. It's the middle of the night so there are only two people who could be calling me—my best friend London or my band manager Archer. If it's London, I'll end up missing him, missing home. If it's Archer...

I reach into my pocket and pull out my phone, my stomach knotting at Archer's image lighting up my screen.

"I've gotta take this real quick," I tell Cooper, shrugging out of his grasp and slinking into a quiet corner to answer the phone.

"Lincoln's in the hospital," Archer says as soon as I answer, confirming my worst fear.

"Is he…?"

"He's alive…for now anyway," he responds grimly.

"What happened?"

"He drank way too much and fell asleep outside on his balcony."

"Fuck," I mutter, remembering how cold it was when I'd gotten to the club. I'd dashed from the car to the door as quickly as possible, glad I wasn't one of the poor saps stuck waiting in line to get inside. I barely even paused for the paparazzi outside, and that's saying something.

"Yeah," Archer agrees with my eloquent assessment of the situation.

"Things are bad, right?" I already know the answer, but I'm hoping like hell Archer will lie to me, tell me everything is going to work out just fine.

"Things are bad," he confirms, and my stomach swoops. "I'll keep you updated on Lincoln, and I'd like to swing by and chat with you tomorrow after everything is settled."

"You got it. I'll be around, so stop by whenever."

"Sounds good. Thanks for being the only one of the guys not giving me gray hair," he manages to joke through his defeated tone.

"My pleasure," I assure him, preening a little under the praise. As long as I'm not a problem, I'm doing my part for the band. As long as I'm always well behaved and wearing my public face, Archer and everyone else will love me.

"I'll talk to you later," he says.

"Later."

I put my phone away, and Cooper tries to wave me back over, but I give him a small shake of my head and an apologetic smile before making a quiet exit.

My car is waiting for me outside, my driver, Tim, jumping out to open the door for me when I get close.

"Calling it an early night?"

"Didn't feel much like partying anymore," I respond vaguely, sliding into the back seat, the cold leather smooth like butter under me. The car smells and feels expensive in every way. It reminds me of what all my hard work has earned for me.

I lean my head against the window as Tim drives me home. The city lights blur past as the cold glass against my forehead sends a chill straight through to my bones. My life is a dream come true—touring the world, having adoring fans, millions of dollars in the bank. So why does it feel so empty sometimes? Why is it the happiest I've ever been was before I was rich and famous? The nights I spent goofing off with London and his twin brother, Paris, *those* were the highlight of my life. Before I was anyone, I was someone in their eyes.

As we near my penthouse apartment, I pull my phone out again and shoot off a text.

Benji: I miss you. I want to come home soon and see you

I don't expect an immediate answer, but it comes anyway.

London: You know where to find me ;)

Some time at home with my parents and best friend sounds like *exactly* what the doctor ordered. I just wonder when I'll be able to fit it in between our crazy tour schedule and Lincoln's frequent near-death experiences. Then again, if the death knell is tolling for Downward Spiral, I'll have plenty of time on my hands before I know it.

I suppose only time will tell.

My doorman greets me with a smile as I shuffle inside and get into the fancy elevator. Leaning against the wall as it makes its ascent to my penthouse, I close my eyes and try to grasp onto the wisps of happiness I felt for a few brief seconds at the club. It's no use though; they're gone, leaving a hollow ache in their place.

The doors ding and open on my floor. I step inside my place and take a deep breath, looking at all the expensive and rare things filling the space. African masks, fertility objects, priceless art, collectible bits of history and culture, they're reminders of all the places I've been and the things I never thought I'd get to see. They're symbols of my success, and right now I'm half-tempted to pull a Jude and rage through my penthouse destroying every last object for failing to live up to their purpose of fulfilling me.

I glare at each item as I pass them but don't do anything to cause any damage, no matter how good it would probably feel.

When I get to my bedroom, I pull my phone out of my pocket and then strip out of my clothes. Crawling between my sheets, I open up Instagram and forgive myself ahead of time for what I'm about to do. I type @ParisJones into the search bar and click on his profile. He hasn't posted in nearly a year, but that doesn't stop me from going back to his account over and over, scrolling through pictures of him happy and smiling, the description and tags encouraging people in the LGBT community to love themselves and don't let anyone tell them they don't belong certain places, and sweet, funny videos of him living his life—working out, talking about whatever issue was on his mind at the time. The last post was from the morning of his injury, the morning before the last game he played.

In the picture, he's in bed, his hair messy, stubble on his cheeks and chin. You can see his boyfriend, Elliot, asleep behind him. The caption for the picture is something about how his team is going to kick some ass in the playoff game scheduled that night and that he'd already promised Elliot that if they won the Super Bowl, he'd take him on a fabulous vacation afterward to make up for all the time spent in the gym or on the field during the season. The picture makes my stomach knot, not just because I'm jealous as hell of the man in his bed, but because it's a reminder of how quickly all your hopes and dreams can come crashing down around you.

I wish I could somehow reach through the screen and warn him of what was about to happen. And I wish I could find a way to go back in time and warn my eighteen-year-old self about all the obstacles in the road ahead. Maybe if I'd known ahead of time, I could've done something to prevent us from going so badly off the rails. I could've smacked the coke out of Jude's hands before he tried it for the first time. I could've kept the razor out of Lincoln's hand the night he nearly killed himself. I could've kept Lando from meeting the guy who broke his heart by never calling again.

When the sun starts to turn the sky a faint pink, I realize how long I've spent staring at pictures of Paris on Instagram, and I set my phone down, pulling my blankets up around my neck and closing my eyes. Maybe if I keep them closed long enough, I'll wake up in an alternate reality where the band I put my blood, sweat, and tears into isn't falling apart.

But no matter how hard I wish for it, I'm not sure there's any saving us.

TRACK 2: SIDE B

Fresh Start

Benji

I clutched the straps of my backpack until my fingers cramped and my knuckles were white, walking down the unfamiliar hallway with my head down and my shoulders hunched. Each shout or boisterous laugh made me flinch, sure it was aimed my way.

I should've cut my hair. I'd spent all summer trying to get up the courage to chop off my long, blond locks, going back and forth between telling myself it would be braver to wear it proudly like I wanted to and knowing it would likely get me beat up again like it always did at my old school. At my old school I'd made up the excuse to myself that it was too late anyway, that even if I cut my hair, wore clothes like everyone else, talked and acted like everyone else, it wouldn't matter because they already *knew*. This school was supposed to be a fresh start, a blank slate to be whoever *wouldn't* end up hiding in broom closets to avoid getting taunted and beaten up.

I saw it in my mother's eyes when I left

the house that morning—pride and worry both swimming in her eyes. She brushed my hair back with her gentle fingers and gave me a kiss on the forehead, telling me to have a good first day at my new school.

I stuttered to a stop when I reached my locker, pulling out the little scrap of paper to double check that it's the right one and then setting my bookbag down by my feet while I tried the combination.

My fingers shook as I turned the lock, carefully entering the combination, acutely aware of everyone around me, sizing up the new kid, making assumptions about me. Admittedly, the assumptions were likely correct, but that didn't make them hurt less.

The combination failed to work the first time, and I whined a little under my breath, wanting to get this done quickly so I could get to my first class and pick a seat in the farthest back corner I could find and start praying the teacher wouldn't make me stand up and introduce myself. I used my index finger to push my glasses back up my nose and read the combination again before giving it another try.

While I tried the combination for a second time, a large, imposing boy took up residence at the locker beside mine. I tensed for a moment, reading *jock* in everything about him from his team jersey to his too-large size for a ninth-grade boy. I glanced at him out of the corner of my eye, still fumbling with my lock, and cringed as I realized he was fucking *hot*.

Great start at a new school, showing up looking like a fag, checking out the jocks. Way to not get your ass kicked again, Benji.

A phantom pain twinged in my ribs, a reminder of what it felt like to be surrounded and kicked until I blacked out. The doctor said I was *lucky* to only have some broken ribs and a collapsed lung. And I guess those boys were lucky it was my word against theirs and the administration decided that wasn't enough to give them any sort of punishment.

The lock finally clicked open, and I breathed a sigh of relief, wrenching it open too hard, the door swinging into the hot jock.

"Oh my god, I'm so sorry," I gasped, scrambling to grab the door and pull it back while my cheeks heated and my heart thundered. Leave it to me to only last five minutes in a new school before getting on someone's bad side.

"You're fine," he assured me with a laugh. I let myself look at him again, *really* look at him this time, and my stomach did a slow roll, my palms growing damp with sweat. His eyes were kind and so was his smile.

When he didn't say anything more, I turned back to my locker, practically shoving my entire head inside to give myself a second to catch my breath and hide my blushing face. The clang of the locker beside me closing was followed by the shrill ring of a bell.

"That's the two-minute warning bell," he explained. "Do you need me to point you in the direction of your first class?"

"N-no thanks," I answered, pushing my glasses up my sweaty nose again, my head still inside my locker.

"Okay, see you around."

See you around, as if we were friends. I was sure it was nothing more than a casual remark. After all, he *would* see me around if our lockers were right next to each other. I just couldn't decide if that was good news or not.

TRACK 3: SIDE A

Get Your Shit Together

Paris

Loud moaning, accompanied by rhythmic thumping, lets me know my neighbor Andy is having a good time...*again*.

I swear, if I'd known I was going to be treated to a constant barrage of porn-worthy noises through the wall, I might've taken London up on his offer to move in with him while I figured shit out rather than getting my own place.

Figured shit out.

It sounds like it would be simple enough, but it feels like my life is one giant clusterfuck right now, emphasis on the *cluster*.

I turn up the volume on the TV to drown out the sound.

"Lead singer of the popular band, Downward Spiral, Lincoln Miller, was reportedly admitted to the emergency room in the early morning hours yester-day," the news anchor says, a picture of the band appearing on the screen.

My breath catches in my chest, the same

way it always does when anyone talks about Downward Spiral or, more specifically, Benji.

I lean forward, turning the TV up even louder, this time not trying to block out Andy's sounds but because I don't want to miss any of the details.

"No details are being offered, but their upcoming tour has been canceled, the band's social media account citing a need for 'down time to recharge'."

The anchor continues to talk and speculate, listing Lincoln's past incidents of suspected self-harm, but all I can do is stare at the smiling picture of Benji. I haven't seen him in person since the night we graduated from high school. My lips tingle at the memory. I absently brush my fingers over them, imagining I can still feel Benji's kiss lingering there, his confession of love hanging between us. A confession of love that wasn't for me, as much as I wanted it to be.

A familiar sense of shame washes over me. I shouldn't feel that way about Benji; I never should've felt that way. He was dating my brother, for fuck sake. Even if they've been broken up for a decade, it doesn't change that fact.

The segment ends, and my breath catches when a picture of my ex flashes across the screen next.

"Actor Elliot Collins has been spotted out and about with a man who is not *his long-time boyfriend, quarterback for the San Diego Scorpions,*

Paris Jones."

"Ugh," I groan. It's not that it's a huge surprise that Elliot is already seeing someone else. Honestly, I would've been more surprised to hear he was still single after three whole weeks. But it still feels like a kick in the stomach to see pictures of him holding hands with his new arm candy.

Things had been rocky between us for a while. Even before my injury things had been going downhill. We were fighting all the time, rarely having sex. It seemed like the only time things felt right was when we were out at one of the parties or social events he loved so much. He's a fame whore, which was the main reason we were together to begin with. But then I got hurt and spent weeks moping around, only getting out of bed for physical therapy, avoiding parties and all the things he loved. Needless to say, he was over it, and I guess so was I.

When I came out, it was front page news for *months*. Becoming the first openly gay pro quarterback in the NFL was more than enough to make me a household name and an icon in the gay community. And I ate that shit up.

Elliot and I met at some posh Hollywood party, the story wasn't really anything noteworthy, just a few too many drinks and a quick fuck in one of the many bedrooms in the vast mansion. He wasn't a big-name actor at the time, not that he's Brad Pitt or anything now.

He'd had a few small roles on different TV shows and movies. Hell, he still hasn't had a major leading role, the only reason the news is even talking about him is because *our* relationship made him someone people cared about.

After we hooked up that night, I didn't expect to hear from him again, but the next day he added me on all his social media profiles, and the flirting started. He'd tweet cute, suggestive things at me, and the Twitterverse would go nuts wondering if we were an item. I'll admit, I enjoyed it as much as he did. Dating him seemed like the right choice.

More people sitting around the news desk speculate about whether Elliot and I broke up or if this other man is just a friend.

"Jesus Christ, don't you people have better things to talk about?" I grumble, switching off the TV and grabbing my phone to text London. I'm bored and restless, in the mood to get out of my too quiet apartment for at least a few hours.

Paris: What are you up to?
London: Just finished up working for the day, thinking about dinner
Paris: Meet at that sandwich place you like?
London: Sounds good

I slip on my shoes and coat, wincing at the pain in my shoulder.

"Fuck," I grumble, pausing to rub at the

23

ache. I can't feel the ugly scar through my coat but it's there, nonetheless.

The horrible popping feeling and the sensation burning through my shoulder and arm as my labrum tore are all still fresh in my mind. It's not like it's been that long, only ten months, but it's like it was a different lifetime ago.

I've been following every instruction from my physical therapist to the letter, but my hopes aren't high. I saw it written in the team doctor's eyes when she told me the diagnosis and recommended surgery. She doesn't think I'll play again, and I'm starting to think I won't either.

Shaking myself out of the endless loop of self-pity, I grab my keys and head out of my apartment.

It's a quick drive to the little deli London loves. Honestly, everywhere in Greenfield is a quick drive because the town is approximately five feet in all directions with twenty residents and no traffic. Okay, *some* of that is an exaggeration, but not by much.

I ask myself nearly every day why I came back to this godforsaken crumb of a town after my life ended. I hated it here growing up, and I still hate it. But after Elliot and I broke up, I couldn't think of anywhere else to go. I didn't want to be all alone in LA, not when I had no reason to be there. Unless and until I get my throwing arm back in shape, there's nothing for me in California.

London is already there waiting for me at a table when I step inside, the little bell of the door chiming to signal my arrival.

"I ordered for you," he tells me as I slide into the seat opposite him, grimacing again when my shoulder aches.

"Shoulder bothering you?"

"I'm fine," I lie.

"Whatever you say, grumpy."

"I'm not grumpy," I argue in a decidedly grumpy tone.

"Okay." He shrugs.

Our sandwiches come up, and I get up to grab them off the counter, plopping London's down in front of him and then digging into my own.

"Did you see that news story about the band?" I ask. I don't have to clarify which band, he already knows. Downward Spiral has always been *the band* to us, or *Benji's band.*

"Mmhmm," he hums and nods while chewing on a large bite of food. "Benji's supposed to give me a call tonight sometime, so I don't know what's going on yet."

My stomach somersaults, and I shove my sandwich into my mouth to hide the gut level reaction any mention of Benji has on me.

"I don't know what's going on with Lincoln, but it's obviously bad if they have to cancel their tour. Between you and me, I don't think

25

that's the worst thing in the world. Benji would never say it, but he's in desperate need of some time off. Plus, I'd love to get a chance to see him. I haven't seen him in person since he came home for Christmas two years ago."

A familiar guilt washes over me listening to London talk about his ex, the man I've had a hopeless crush on since the minute I laid eyes on him fifteen years ago. And, not to split hairs, but I totally saw him first.

Benji

It's late in the afternoon by the time Archer knocks on my door. I spent most of the morning taking all my frustration and uncertainty out on my piano, bleeding my emotions into music rather than sitting with them. I'd considered calling London, but the ache of missing home was too much, and I knew talking to my best friend would only make it worse. Instead, I texted him that I'd call him sometime tonight, because I have a feeling I'm going to need to after I talk with Archer.

Of all the things I didn't expect when I imagined Downward Spiral's success, it was how lonely it would be.

"Hey Arch, how's Lincoln doing?" I ask, stepping aside to let Archer in. His eyes flicker over my various collectables as he comes inside, and a smile forms on his lips. I can visibly see some of the tension ease from his shoulders, and I give myself a mental pat on the back. *I'm the easy one; I'm the one without any problems.*

"Lincoln is...Lincoln," Archer answers with a sigh.

Our lead singer's struggle with self-harm isn't anything new. I didn't know about it before we signed the record contract, as far as I know no one did, but it became clear very quickly. While Jude jumped head first into coke and sex, Lincoln withdrew from everyone and nurtured his pain until it grew so big it overtook him.

The call from Archer all those years ago, frantic and horrified as he told us Lincoln was on the way to the hospital, still stars in many of my nightmares. I can remember the dried blood on Archer's clothes and the haunted look in his eyes when I got to the hospital. I thought Lincoln was gone, and he pretty damn near was.

And what was Lincoln's response after nearly bleeding out on his bathroom floor? Write a hit song about it, of course. "Crimson Tiles" got us a Grammy, and in some ways, it felt like giving away a piece of our souls. He promised it wouldn't happen again, and, to his credit, it hasn't, at least not to that extent. But that doesn't mean we don't all notice the scabs and scars, the bloody razor blades left on the bathroom sink in the tour bus.

"Is he still in the hospital? What did the doctor say?" I ask.

"He's at home, and the doctor said he made it through everything okay *this time*, but I'm starting to worry that he's not going to quit until he finishes the job."

"We have to do something. I've always figured at some point he'd get his shit together eventually, but if anything, I feel like he's getting worse." I roll my bottom lip between my teeth, furrowing my brows as I make this confession to Archer, afraid he'll balk at my concern, tell me to leave the worrying to him like he has in the past.

"I agree. Which is why I think you all need a vacation. I've canceled the tour and talked to Lando. I'm going to give Lincoln a couple days before I spring the news on him though. And I'm not going to bother giving Jude a chance to weigh in; he needs help, and I'm already arranging it for him whether he likes it or not."

His words surprise me, but they also put a smile on my face, a light feeling filling my chest as I realize that instead of cramming onto the tour bus again in a few days, I'll be able to go home instead.

"A vacation sounds nice. I'd love to go home for a little while, see my parents and London."

A flicker of a knowing smirk crosses Archer's face, and I know he's thinking what everyone thinks: that there's something more between London and me than simple friendship. So we used to fuck around? Last time I checked that wasn't marriage. He's my best friend in the world, and I'm a little tired of defending it, so I don't bother.

"I'm meeting with someone tomorrow to help with Jude. If we're going to take a break, then I want to try to get him help. I'm going to do everything I can to save this band."

"Thanks, Arch. You're a great manager."

He scoffs and shakes his head. "If that were true, I would've done something about Jude and Lincoln long before now."

"Those two are like trains jumping the track; there's only so much one person can do."

"Well, I'm going to do better from here on out, you can bet on that."

He doesn't linger after the announcement, telling me he'll book me a flight home by the end of the week and send me over the details. I do a little dance in the hallway once he gets back on the elevator and the doors close. I'm going to be home for Christmas instead of on a cramped tour bus with the smell of dirty socks and ball sweat permeating the air. I'll get to wake up Christmas morning and have breakfast with my parents instead of watching Lincoln out of the corner of my eye to see if he's hurting himself or counting the number of times Jude "goes to the bathroom", which we all know is code for stuffing his nose full of drugs.

I pull out my phone and dial my mom.

"Hi sweetie," she answers right away. "I

saw that awful story about Lincoln. Is he okay?"

"You know how Lincoln is," I answer vaguely. "I have some good news though."

"What's that?"

"The tour was canceled; I'm coming home for Christmas."

"Oh, that's wonderful news!" She sounds as giddy as I feel. "When will you be home?"

"By the end of the week. I'll let you know the flight details once I have them."

"Great, I'll pick you up from the airport," she says. "I'm so happy I get to spend Christmas with my favorite son."

"I'm your only son, Mom," I remind her with a laugh.

"As far as *you* know," she teases.

I laugh, and we end up chatting a little longer before we hang up with promises to talk soon.

Sometimes I feel bad that I hit the jackpot when it came to my parents while Lincoln and Jude were stuck with such sorry excuses for them. I had my fair share of bullshit to deal with growing up, but my parents always had my back. When I got bullied, they raised hell to get me switched to a new school. When I sat at home crying about not having any friends, they listened and told me one day things would get better. And when I told them I was gay, they smiled and hugged me.

After hanging up with my mom, I wander

into my living room and plop down on my couch to call London. The conversation with him is more or less the same, shared excitement when I tell him I'll be home in a few days and then idle chat about our lives for a while.

Sometimes I wish I *did* love London as more than a friend, because nothing would be easier. But as much fun as we had getting off together as teenagers, there's just no spark.

"You know, you're coming home at an *excellent* time. Paris is on the rebound, and he's been super mopey. I think the two of you banging it out would do you both some good."

"You do realize your investment in me fucking your brother is getting a bit creepy, right?" I deadpan.

"What's creepy about it? I care about both of you and want you to be happy."

"Well, he's not the least bit interested in me, so I doubt he'd want to rebound with me. The only reason he hung around me in high school was because I practically lived at your house. And I've conveniently not seen him even once since then."

"I'm going to make sure you two see each other this time, and I'll bet you twenty bucks some sparks fly."

I snort a laugh. "Oh sweetie, that's adorable. You do realize I find hundreds in my couch cushions, right?"

"Fine, I bet you a thousand dollars sparks

fly," he says.

"Okay, but don't think I'm not going to take your money. You might not make rock star money, but I know for a fact you make bank designing those websites, and you live in Greenfield, so your rent is probably about fifty bucks a month."

"Fair enough," London laughs. "I can't wait to see you, man."

"Same. I'll call you as soon as I'm in town."

"Looking forward to it."

We hang up, and I stretch out on my ridiculously expensive couch with a smile on my face. I know the band is in trouble; I know having to cancel the tour is a bad thing. But right now, I can't find it in me to care. All I want is to leave all this bullshit behind for a little while and spend some time with the people I love.

TRACK 4: SIDE B

Pretty Boys

Paris

The tap, tap, tap of my pen against my notebook was no doubt annoying to everyone sitting around me, trying to listen to the teacher go over the syllabus for the semester. But unease and confusion were raging through me like a storm; if I didn't tap, I thought I might end up fizzing over like a shaken soda.

He was new here, that much I was sure of. If I'd seen him before, I would've remembered it. When I first got to my locker and his back was to me, I thought he was a girl. My eyes had latched onto the way his tight jeans molded around his nicely shaped butt. The strangest urge to reach out and cup the shapely cheeks had come over me, and my first thought was *finally! After two years of faking it with my friends, there's a girl I find hot!*

My eyes had traveled up the rest of his body, drinking in the slim, straight lines of his hips and the wide set of his shoulders. Maybe that should've given away the fact that *he* was not a *she*. But the flowing blond hair had tricked me, lured me in and tricked me into checking out a guy.

When I squeezed in beside him and sneaked a peek at his face, my heart stopped for a second before taking off in a gallop, lodging itself in my throat at the same time.

His eyes had darted in my direction in a sideways glance like he was afraid to get caught looking at me. I noticed his fingers were trembling as he fumbled with his lock. I wanted to offer to help him get it open, to tell him these lockers were old and shitty, often requiring special tricks to get them open. But my body was on fire and my brain was still fixated on the shape of his butt.

When he finally wrenched his locker open and the door swung so hard it clanged against my shoulder, I was able to snap myself out of my stupor long enough to feign politeness. But as soon as I got to my class and sat down, the entirety of the situation washed over me.

I couldn't like guys. I'd been playing football since I was eight and was likely going to make varsity next year—the coach was that impressed with my throwing arm. I liked to work out and watch sports. I couldn't like guys.

"You okay, man?" my friend, Randy, asked from behind me.

"Great," I lied.

I would avoid going to my locker this year,

I decided. I could keep my books in my backpack at all times, and then I wouldn't have to see him and his pretty hair and nice butt. If I didn't have to see him, I'm sure this would all blow over.

My mom said I was a late bloomer when it came to girls, and I was sure she was right. Any day I'd find a girl much prettier than that boy.

With a solid plan in place, I took a deep breath and focused my attention back on the front of the room.

Benji

I made it through seven classes, including lunch, without any incidents. I kept my head down and avoided talking or making eye contact with anyone. It was lonely, but much, much safer than the alternative.

Then, I stepped into my English class and skidded to a halt. This class was on the other side of the building from my seventh period class, so I was cutting it close, which meant there was only one open seat left. One seat in the back row, right beside the handsome boy with the nice smile.

I tightened my grip on the strap of my backpack and scurried over to slide into the empty seat. I was right below the clock on the wall so I could hear the steady beat of the ticks. I latched onto it and listened for other sounds in the room—the chatter of other students, the clicking of pens, the tapping of feet—making it all into a melody in my mind, effectively easing my nerves...until *he* noticed me. He gave me a friendly smile I couldn't manage to return thanks to the nerves fluttering in my stomach making me feel like I might vomit any second.

I studiously pulled out my pencil and notebook, letting my hair fall forward to create a curtain between the two of us.

"I like your hair," he said quietly, almost shyly. It was different than how he sounded earlier, and it occurred to me his clothes were different too. He wasn't wearing a jersey anymore; he was wearing a red t-shirt.

"Thanks," I responded in a small voice before clearing my throat and brushing my hair back so I could see him better. "Did you change your clothes?"

He cocked his head and raised his eyebrows at me. After a few seconds, understanding dawned in his eyes.

"Did you meet my brother, Paris?"

"Um...maybe? I didn't get his name, but his locker is right next to mine."

"Looked exactly like me except he was wearing some football shirt and a pair of ratty gym shoes?"

"Yeah."

"Yup, that's Paris. No one can ever tell us apart," he confessed, and I could hear a hint of resentment in his voice. "Even though he's Mr. Popular Jock and I'm...not." He huffed out a breath and rolled his eyes, and instantly, I liked him. Not the way I *liked* his brother, but in a way that made me feel comfortable, like we could be friends. I'd never had a friend before, not really. It seemed like it would be nice. In fact, in that moment, I thought I might do just about anything to make sure he liked me enough to want to be my friend.

"I'm London, by the way," he introduced himself.

"Benji," I said. "Do you...um..." I drew a blank. *What did kids my age like to do? Probably not spend their entire afternoon playing piano or violin, right?*

"Probably not," he said with a laugh before I could continue floundering. "You're new here, so I'll save you some trouble and tell you now. I'm captain of the Math Club and first chair tuba in the school band. I'm not cool or popular, and I don't do most things other people consider fun."

The last bit of tension eased from my shoulders, and I gave him a genuine smile this time.

"I play piano and violin, and I had to leave my last school because kids wouldn't stop beating me up."

Sympathy flashed across his face, his eyes darting over me, no doubt figuring out in an instant exactly why I kept getting the shit kicked out of me.

"I probably would too if it wasn't for my brother."

The mention of his brother made my face heat.

"At least you're not scrawny like me," I pointed out. In fact, for a self-proclaimed nerd, he was as built as his brother was.

"Yeah, Paris lets me workout with him," he explained.

"That must be nice."

I always wished I could have a brother, someone who would always be around to spend time with.

He just shrugged. Then the teacher started talking, and our conversation had to end. But I couldn't keep myself from sneaking looks at London every so often during class. Was it possible I'd made my first friend?

TRACK 5: SIDE A

Home Sweet Home

Benji

I filled my Gucci luggage full of name brand clothes and expensive toiletries. Then made some social media posts about the much-needed vacation the band is taking. Archer told me I didn't need to maintain my own social media accounts. In fact, none of the other guys do, but I like it. I like getting to read comments and posts from fans telling me how much they love me, how much we inspire them, or that our music has gotten them through difficult times.

A few weeks ago there was a post from a teenage boy saying he was bullied at school a lot for being gay, but that seeing how successful and famous we are made him believe things would get better for him one day. That post alone was worth more than every dollar in my substantial bank account. After I saw that post, I wrote a letter to him and put a check with a lot of zeros on it into an envelope and gave it to Archer to send to the kid. I have more money than I know what to do with anyway; it's better given away than spent on more useless junk.

I look around at all the rare and collectible items lining my walls and feel a familiar hollowness in my chest. What the fuck is any of this even about? What am I doing here in this overpriced apartment with all this junk I don't really care about? I have money so I spend it on all these things to make my too big penthouse feel cozier and to impress other people. It's shallow, and I hate it. But I can't seem to let it go.

My phone rings, my doorman calling to tell me my car is waiting to take me to Lincoln's. I don't know why I thought I could get out of New York without some big goodbye scene, but Archer stomped those dreams when he sent me my travel itinerary and followed it up by telling me all the guys would meet at Lincoln's before my car would take me to the airport.

The ride to Lincoln's is quick, seeing that he only lives a few blocks away, but as I stand in the elevator watching the floor numbers light up as they pass, a surreal feeling washes over me. This might be the last time the four of us all stand in a room together—as bandmates or otherwise. I'm not naive enough to think the label is cool with us canceling a tour on short notice like this. And I haven't missed all the signs written on the walls in the past year— Jude's drug use, Lincoln's self-harm, and Lando's inability to write any more music. We're due to sign a new contract with Epic Records soon, and something tells me that's not going to happen. This little vacation we're taking is more than likely going to be permanent.

I step off the elevator to find Lando and Jude already there along with Archer.

I give a casual smile, doing my best not to betray all the emotions crashing inside me like waves. Jude is scowling, Lando looks exhausted, and Archer seems to be holding his nerves together by a thread. I can be the one who keeps cool. I can be the one without any problems or worries if that's what they all need from me.

"Well, let's do this," I encourage, leading the way toward Lincoln's bedroom, my bandmates falling into step beside me.

The discussion goes about as well as I would've expected—Lincoln getting defensive, Jude getting pissed, tension and all the things we don't say to each other creating a distance between us I think we all resent. It was never supposed to be like this. There was a time we were closer than brothers, and now it's like we hardly know each other anymore.

I leave Lincoln's place feeling even worse about the prospect of the band making it through this time off intact. The thought of losing my music chokes me. It's not perfect, but this is my fucking dream, and to think it could all slip away is too much to consider.

*****

The small, regional airport in the middle of nowhere Ohio fills me with a sense of home in a way nothing in New York ever can.

I spot my mom waiting for me near baggage claim, and a weight immediately eases off my shoulders, a smile tugging at my lips. Striding over to her, I scoop her up into my arms and give her a fierce hug.

"I missed you," I say before setting her down.

"Well, it wouldn't kill you to visit more," she teases.

"I wish I could. It feels like I never have a minute to breathe lately, always on tour or in the studio," I complain, allowing myself to drop my *everything's perfect* persona for a split second.

"Oh honey, if there's too much on your plate, you should tell someone."

"Everything's fine," I lie, snapping back into a reassuring smile. "Let me grab my bag, and we can get home so you can feed me.

"You *are* looking awfully skinny," she comments, giving my arm a squeeze. "Are you eating?"

"I eat," I assure her.

"You need a haircut," she fusses next as I pull my bag off the conveyor belt. I know a lot of people find it irritating when their parents worry over them, but I don't mind it. I know it's her way of showing she cares, so I'm happy to take each bit of criticism and mothering she can throw my way.

"My hair is fine."

She tsks. "Just a trim. I can do it in five minutes."

"No offense, Mom, but I spend more on hair products and stylists every year than your house cost, so I'm not going to let a crazy lady with a pair of kitchen scissors start hacking away at it."

She tsks again. "That's just silly."

"I agree. You should've let me buy you that bigger house I wanted to get you so you wouldn't be living in such a cheap place."

"I happen to like our house."

"I like your house too," I admit, slinging one arm over her shoulder once I've grabbed my bag, and steer her toward the exit.

Paris

"You've got it, one more rep," my physical therapist, Krista, encourages.

I grunt and pull my arm up one more time with the ten-pound weight in my hand. My muscle trembles, and my shoulder burns. I grit my teeth with frustration as I fall short of completing the rep before dropping the weight on the floor and cursing loudly.

"This is bullshit; I can lift ten times that weight in my sleep."

"Paris." Krista says my name in that scolding tone she's so good at. "We've talked about this; we're building your strength back up. You can't keep beating yourself up about not being able to do what you used to."

"It doesn't feel like I'm getting any stronger."

"You did more reps than last week," she points out.

"One and a half more reps."

"It's still an improvement."

"Not enough of an improvement. I'm supposed to be ready for training camp in *four* months if I'm going to play this season." I can hear the panic and desperation creeping into my voice, and I hate myself for it. My heart beats faster, and I clench my fists and my jaw. "Give it to me straight; is there any chance I'm going to be ready?"

She gives me a look full of pity, and I want to hit something. "I don't know."

I've been working my ass off, doing *exactly* what she's told me to do every step of the way, and it feels like I'm trying to run in quicksand.

"You're doing everything in your power, keep reminding yourself of that," she says reassuringly. "You're only human, and you can only do what's within your body's limitations. I think right now the thing holding you back more than anything is the pressure you're putting on yourself. Maybe you'll be ready in time, maybe you won't, but beating yourself up isn't going to make the difference."

"Yeah," I grumble an agreement.

"It's the holidays; why don't you take some time to relax, do something for yourself."

"I'll try," I agree. I can't imagine anything I'd *want* to do for myself. The only thing I want is to wake up with my shoulder magically better.

"Take care of yourself, Paris, emotionally as well as physically," Krista advises. "Now, I've got another appointment to get ready for, so I'll see you in January, right?"

"Right." I pick up the weight I dropped and put it back on the rack before heading into the locker room to get changed.

TRACK 6: SIDE B

Strange New Feelings

Paris

I groaned and pulled my pillow over my head at the sound of my brother's tuba. I'd slept like shit all week, and the *one* thing I wanted to do was sleep in on Saturday. My plan to avoid going to my locker was working, but somehow that wasn't keeping that boy out of my mind. Thoughts of him were keeping me up at night and plaguing my mind during the day. I found myself looking around for him at school while at the same time avoiding going to my locker where I knew he would be. All the confusion was making me sick to my stomach.

And my pain in the ass brother decided to wake me up before noon on a Saturday...I was going to have to kill him and bury his body in the backyard. It would be fine. I could pretend to be both of us, and no one would ever know the difference.

I threw my covers back and marched out of my room in nothing but my boxers, intent on telling London off. My footsteps thundered as I stomped down the hallway to his bedroom and flung open the door. I opened my mouth to bark my annoyance and instead, found my voice dying in my dry throat.

My mouth flapped open and closed like a fish as *his* eyes landed on me. Surprise, then fear, then embarrassment flicked through them in quick succession until he dipped his head.

"Dude, would you mind not standing in my bedroom naked while I have a friend here?" London chided.

"Friend?" I repeated stupidly.

"Don't sound so shocked; I can make a friend," he defended. "This is Benji. He's new at school, and he's my friend."

"Benji." I must have sounded like an idiot, repeating everything my brother said. I looked at *Benji* again, taking in his silky hair, delicate yet masculine features, and slim frame, and my body heated in response. Now I had a name to go along with my crush, and that was undoubtedly what this was. I had a crush on Benji, and I didn't have the first clue what to make of that.

"We were going to play videogames; do you want to play with us?" Benji offered in a small, timid voice that didn't seem to fit him at all. I wanted to hear how he sounded when he was relaxed and having fun. I wanted to know what his laugh was like.

"Yeah, I'll play," I agreed.

"Maybe you should put some pants on first," London grumbled, clearly irritated with me. I wasn't sure why he was mad, though. Was it because Benji was his friend first, and I was horning in on their hanging out? Or was it possible...

I looked at my brother, studying him as if I'd somehow be able to tell if he could possibly like Benji the way *I* liked Benji. Was it possible London was...*gay*? Was *I*?

"Actually, I forgot I have plans with the guys from the team," I lied, the urge to get as far away from Benji as possible rushing over me.

"Okay, see ya," London waved me away dismissively, but I caught a hint of disappointment in Benji's eyes.

"Maybe next time?" he suggested, twirling a strand of his long hair around his index finger nervously.

"Maybe," I muttered before turning and bolting from the room as fast as I could.

TRACK 7: SIDE A

Truth Hurts
Paris

When my phone rings with a number I don't recognize, I consider ignoring it, but then I think *what the hell* and answer it anyway, even knowing it's more than likely some gossip columnist calling to ask about Elliot and me.

"Hello?"

"Hi, is this Paris?" The man on the other end asks.

"Yes, who's this?"

"This is Malcolm...Malcolm Tanner."

It takes me several seconds to figure out why I know that name, and then it hits me, he's the guy Elliot's been seen all around with recently.

"If you're calling to ask how to get Elliot to clean up after his damn self, then I can tell you now that's hopeless," I joke through my heart in my throat. Why the fuck is Elliot's new boyfriend calling *me*?

He gives a weak chuckle. "No, I just wanted to assure you that the stories aren't true."

"You're *not* dating Elliot?"

"No, I am," he says. "But a lot of articles and things today are saying that Elliot was cheating on you with me."

I grit my teeth. I'd been avoiding reading or listening to most of the gossip, but I *had* seen that little tidbit. I'd chalked it up to clickbait, but I can't deny I had wondered a bit.

"He wasn't cheating with you?" I check.

"No, we've only been together eight months."

My stomach drops, and I clench my phone harder in my hand. I'm not sure what to say or do until a scoffing laugh escapes my lips.

"The fact that Elliot and I were living together up until about three weeks ago didn't give you a hint that he wasn't single eight months ago?"

"He said you guys were basically already broken up," Malcolm rushes to explain. "He told me you both knew it was over but were afraid to make it official because you'd been together so long."

"Right," I mutter and shake my head, even though he can't see me. "Good luck with all that."

I click the end button before I can make a fool of myself by yelling, or worse, crying, to Elliot's new boyfriend. Although, apparently, he's not *that* new, since they've been together nearly a year.

That fucking shithead was fucking some buffed out, up-and-coming baseball star for *months* while I was recovering from surgery and fighting like hell every day to get my ass out of bed instead of wallowing over my injury. While my life felt like it was falling apart, he thought the best thing he could do for me was go stick his dick in someone else.

My mind races over the past four years, and I start to wonder if Malcolm was the only one. Things were rough between us for a while. What was Elliot doing while I read every save-your-relationship book I could find? Whose bed was he in while I planned weekend getaways and bought toys to spice up our sex life? I did everything I could think of to make things work, and the whole time he had already moved on without bothering to tell me.

My fists clench, the temptation to plow them into a wall is almost too much to resist. I grind my teeth so hard I'm sure I'm about to crack one. Unsure what else to do, I send a text to London to find out where he is, and when he sends back the name of a bar just outside town, I'm in my shoes and coat in record time.

Once I'm outside, some of the rage fog clears. Instead of heading for my car like I originally planned, I order an Uber instead. I'm going to get drunk as hell tonight goddammit.

The bar London told me to meet him at isn't one I've ever been to. When I step inside,

I'm surprised to realize it's a piano bar. Not exactly a place I pictured my math nerd brother.

I spot him at a booth near the large piano, which sits on a small raised platform in the middle of the room. He waves at me, holding up a martini glass and smiling. Oh, for the love of god, this is *so* not going to cut it tonight.

I make my way over to him, shaking my head before I even reach him.

"We need to go to a real bar," I complain as soon as I'm standing in front of my brother.

He frowns and takes a sip of his drink. "But this is so fancy. Besides, there's a surprise coming up soon."

"A surprise?" I ask with raised eyebrows. "I'm serious, London. I need to get completely shitfaced right now, and some fancy martinis aren't going to do the trick."

He frowns at me. "What happened?"

"I just found out Elliot had been cheating on me."

London's eyes go wide with horror. "Shit, those stories were true?"

"Yup," I say waving down a waitress and slipping into the seat next to him. Since he's not making any effort to get up and take me to a real bar, I guess I'll have to do my best to get drunk here in the meantime.

Before the conversation can go any further, the lights dim, and a spotlight illuminates the piano. *Oh, just fucking great, now I'm going to*

*have to listen to some old motherfucker croon away
while playing the piano.*

"Lon, can we please—"

"Shh," he scolds, his eyes trained on the stage with a glimmer of excitement.

A man moves through the crowd, drawing interested whispers from patrons, and once he comes into view, I can see why. With a black mask around his eyes, he has a real *Phantom of the Opera* vibe as he climbs onto the piano platform. He has blond hair, pulled back into a bun at the back of his head, and a hint of a smile on his pink, bowed lips. He's wearing a fancy tux, which seems over the top, even for this crowd. It feels more like a performance piece than anything.

But his odd appearance is completely forgotten, a hush falling over the crowd, myself included, as he starts to play. His fingers move over the keys with fluid, effortless movements, giving the impression he could play perfectly even in his sleep. The songs flow from one classical piece to the next, all of which are familiar but that I couldn't name if my life depended on it. It's exactly what I imagined someone would play at a piano bar, and yet nothing like it at the same time. I didn't expect to feel emotions swelling inside me along with tears. I didn't expect to be moved by the music created out of thin air by this talented man's fingers.

My eyes are glued to his face. Even with

some of his face obscured, the pure ecstasy in his expression pulls me in and refuses to release me.

As he plays, the tempo changes and instead of classical, I catch the beat of a few modern pop songs mixed in. His eyes open and meet mine over the piano. I gasp at the familiar, ice blue eyes sparkling with mischief. He winks and heat licks at my skin.

"Benji," I whisper.

"He's amazing, right?" London says, smiling up at his friend. "Sometimes I forget all the raw talent that's hiding under his flashy, rock star persona."

I swallow against my dry throat and nod before taking a sip of the drink I ordered. I've spent the last ten years carefully avoiding running into Benji again, and now here we are. On tonight of all nights, when I'm more vulnerable than I've ever been.

Benji

Paris looks better than ever. Don't get me wrong; the varsity quarterback was the star of *every* teen fantasy I had. But it's clear he's grown into quite the man, too. He didn't peak in high school like some Prom Kings do.

I glance over at my best friend and give him a stern look. I can't believe he didn't tell me he invited Paris tonight. A little warning would've been nice before having to look my former crush in the eye and try desperately not to turn back into the awkward nerd I was back then. London just smirks and shrugs. The little shit.

Back in high school the two of them lived up to the *identical* part of being identical twins. Even though Paris was the jock and London was a total nerd, he used to work out with his brother, so he was fairly bulky back then too. They went to different colleges, and London fell off his habit of lifting weights, but it's clear Paris didn't. Aside from muscles, London now sports a sensible haircut and proper *adult* wardrobe, whereas Paris seems to still be going for Frat Boy chic. I can't lie; the frat boy look is working for me.

I give the final keystrokes an extra flourish and then stand to give a quick bow to the audience. The mask likely wasn't necessary based on the demographics of the audience tonight, but it was fun anyway.

I hop off the small stage and beeline straight for London and Paris, seated in the nearest booth. I paste on my best cool, confident smile and slide into the seat beside London, reaching for his martini and taking a sip.

"Great job," he says, giving me a quick, friendly kiss on the cheek.

London and I spent most of high school getting into each other's pants, but for us, it was never anything more than mutual exploration and a bit of fun. I love him, but only as a friend, and I know he feels the same way. If I ever doubted it, the fact that he's constantly trying to get me together with his brother is a dead giveaway.

"Hey, Paris," I greet casually. "Long time, no see." Ten years to be exact. In fact, the last time I saw him I was drunkenly kissing him.

"Very long time," he agrees.

"How have you been?"

Paris lets out a humorless laugh and throws back the rest of his drink before flagging down the waitress. "Been better," he mutters.

"Yeah, back up, so Elliot was fucking some minor league baseball player while you were still together?" London asks his brother, clearly picking up the thread of a conversation I missed the beginning of.

"Apparently," Paris responds dryly.

"That's fucked up," I say, offering him a sympathetic look.

"You know what you should do," London says, a wicked glint lighting his eyes, making me completely sure I'm going to hate his suggestion. "You should get a really impressive boyfriend and parade him around for the news to see. It would fucking *kill* Elliot to see you with someone more famous than he could get."

"Oh, right, why didn't I think of that? I'll just pick out one of the very eligible bachelors banging down my door and use him to make my ex jealous." He throws in an eye roll to let his brother know just how stupid he finds the suggestion.

"No, any old guy won't do," London continues undeterred. "You need someone super hot, totally rich, and legit famous." He takes a victory sip from his martini.

"If you find a guy like that who wants to date me, send him my way."

London turns to me with a pointed look.

"Me?" My face heats as Paris whips his gaze over toward me as well.

"Benji? I can't date Benji," Paris says in a hurry, taking me instantly back to being an awkward teenager all over again. *Obviously,* Paris doesn't want to date me, but that doesn't make it suck any less to hear it out loud.

"So, fake date him," London says with a shrug. "Make some Instagram posts together, get photographed in public looking adorable together."

"As mature as that sounds, I don't think it's the best idea."

"Why not?" London presses.

"Because he's…he…" Paris struggles to say whatever it is that I apparently am that makes the idea of even *pretending* to like me too much to bear.

"Leave your brother alone, Donnie," I admonish.

"I hate when you call me Donnie," he complains, sticking a finger into his drink and flicking a few droplets at me.

"I know, and Paris hates it when you come up with harebrained ideas, so drop it."

"Fiiiiiine."

"Thank you," Paris says, his eyes flicking to mine with a gratitude. "Now, can we go somewhere to get some *real* drinks because I need to get shitfaced."

"I'm in," I agree, pulling out my phone. "Hold on, let me find out what bar is the most highly rated nearby."

"I don't really care if it's highly rated, as long as it has alcohol."

"Let him do it," London advises. "If he doesn't get to pick out the most hipster, amazing place he can find, he'll spend the whole night pouting about it."

"If you're going to do something, do it right," I defend. "Okay, I found one, and I ordered us a car that should be here in five minutes."

TRACK 8: SIDE B

No Denying

Paris

I was sixteen, and there was no doubt about it, I was gay. I'd been pretty sure for the past few years, more or less since I met Benji. But watching him stand in the bright, summer sun, putting his long hair up into a bun on the top of his head, his lean torso on full display, his swim trunks slung low on his hips, had my sixteen-year-old libido going wild.

London walked over to him and casually slung a shoulder over Benji's shoulder. My blood boiled, and the muscle in my jaw ticked. Why did my brother get to touch him so casually? So freely? My gut ached with wanting him sometimes, and it had only gotten worse the past few months.

No one was surprised when Benji came out. You only had to spend about two minutes with the guy to know he was gay. But there was something about him saying it openly that made it all the harder to keep my own secret.

Benji turned into London and bit his

shoulder playfully, causing a little tussle that ended with them both dragging each other over the edge, splashing loudly into the water.

My stomach twisted again and I couldn't help but hate my brother a little. It probably wasn't fair of me to hate him, after all I had all the things most teenagers could possibly want— popularity, attention from girls, tons of friends, and aspiration. But I didn't have the one thing that London had...*Benji*.

London came out right after Benji, with his best friend right by his side when he told our parents. They were surprised...hell, so was I, but after the initial shock, they assured him they loved him no matter what and so did I. That was when my gnawing jealousy started. I wanted to tell them too; I didn't want to keep hiding and pretending. But I also knew it was a very different thing for the star quarterback to come out than a couple of band nerds.

Then, last week, I walked in on the two of them fooling around in London's bedroom. They were too wrapped up in what they were doing to notice me walking in and quickly back out, but I certainly got an eyeful. I had wondered off and on if there was something between them, but I comforted myself by deciding they were only friends. That was a lot harder to convince myself of after I'd seen Benji's hand down my brother's pants.

The two of them splashing in the pool and

laughing drew my attention again as I watched from the kitchen window feeling every bit the outsider I was.

Benji

We climbed out of the pool, dripping all over the deck without a care in the world.

"You think your parents will let you sleep over?" London asked as he tossed me a towel.

I shrugged and then started to dry off. "I don't see why not. It's summer; they shouldn't care."

"Awesome. We can stay up late playing video games…and stuff."

"And stuff," I agreed with a grin, my eyes catching a flicker of movement at the kitchen window.

"Is it just me, or is Paris being really weird lately?" London asked, following my gaze to where his brother was not-so-sneakily watching us.

"Do you think it's the gay thing?" I asked, nibbling my bottom lip and turning my back to the window.

"I don't *think* so. I mean, he hasn't said any-thing homophobic or whatever."

I nodded noncommittally. I wasn't so sure Paris wasn't freaked out about the gay thing. The way I'd seen him looking at me since I came out was…strange. His eyes always seemed to be on me, sometimes bordering on hostile, other times it was harder to tell.

But even his odd behavior did nothing to stem the crush I had on him.

Most people couldn't tell London and Paris apart by appearance, but I had no trouble at all. True, they had the same haircut, eye color, face shape, and even body type, but they carried themselves too differently; it was easy to pick out who was who. Maybe it was because I spent so much time with London, and so much time pinning for Paris, but I thought I knew them better than anyone. And one thing I'd noticed in the past year or so was that Paris had a secret.

He'd always been this outgoing, confident guy. I doubted anyone had even noticed the change in him except for me, because he did a great job of faking it, but I'd noticed him drawing into himself more, faking smiles instead of meaning them.

"What are you thinking about so hard?" London asked, studying my face curiously.

"Nothing," I lied.

"It's about Paris, isn't it?" he guessed, and I could feel myself blushing. "It's always about Paris," he concluded with a sigh.

"Sorry," I muttered.

"Can I ask you a weird question?" London asked, chewing his bottom lip. I nodded and braced myself. I had a feeling I knew exactly what he was going to ask. "When we, *you know*..." He flicked his eyes to my junk to make sure I got what he was referring to. "Well, are you thinking about Paris?"

"No. I mean, I like Paris and everything, but I'm not like, doing stuff with you just because you look like him."

Tension visibly eased off London's shoulders. "Okay, good, because that would be weird. I mean, I know we don't like each other *that way*, but it would be weird if you were thinking about my brother when we were...*you know*."

"We're friends; I wouldn't use you like that," I promised him.

"I know."

TRACK 9: SIDE A

Too Much to Drink

Paris

I can't believe my brother suggested I pretend to date his ex. I cast a glance at Benji out of the corner of my eye as our shoulders brush against each other in the backseat of the Uber. My entire body feels like it's heating up, awareness of his presence prickling along my skin, making every hair on my arm stand on end. I want to press closer to him, to put my arm around him and kiss him again just to see if it could possibly be as good as I remember.

I haven't seen Benji in person in ten years; you'd think he'd have lost the power to affect me this way by now.

When he'd said the bar was nearby, he was clearly using that term very generously, because it takes nearly an hour to reach our destination. The bar he picked is about as trendy as you can get for Ohio, and the longing to get the hell out of this state washes over me again. I didn't love the spotlight the way Elliot did, but there's something entirely too sad about the thought of my biography ending with me wasting away in the middle of nowhere after my career ending injury. The problem is what the fuck am I sup- posed to do now? I don't really belong anywhere. I don't have any skills or interests outside of football. I dedicated my entire life to my sport, and it was snatched away from me in a fraction of a second.

"Come on, you clearly need a drink," Benji says, clapping me on the shoulder and shoving me toward the bar.

"That's an understatement," I agree, ask- ing the bartender for a beer and a dozen shots of tequila.

"Fucking hell, I'm going to regret this in the morning," London complains, reaching for one of the shots as soon the bartender brings them over.

"Live a little," Benji chides my brother, taking two shots for himself and downing them one after the other in rapid succession.

"Fine," London tilts his head back, swal- lowing the alcohol and reaching for another one. "Let's have a toast," he suggests, and Benji and I both grab another shot to toast with. "To new beginnings."

Something sad passes through Benji's eyes before turning to a hard determination.

"To new beginnings," he agrees tapping his shot glass to mine and then to London's and all three of us drink.

*****

The car stops in front of my apartment building, and Benji practically climbs onto my lap to get out faster.

"Dude, where are you going?" London asks, laughing at Benji's drunk ass stumbling out of the car.

"I have to pee *so* bad. I can use your bathroom, right Pear Bear?"

"Only if you *never* call me Pear Bear again," I bargain.

"Deal, now let's go before I pee my pants and end up on the cover of some magazine with my pants wet."

"We're in the middle of bum fuck Ohio; *how* would a magazine get a picture of you with pee pants?"

"You think your brother wouldn't snap a picture and sell it for a cool half-mil?" he reasons.

"I so would," London agrees, and I laugh.

"Fair enough. Hell, for half a million I'd cut off your hand and send it to a magazine."

"As long as you don't cut my hair," Benji says, hopping from one foot to the other in an exaggerated pee dance, while also swaying from all the drinks he knocked back through the night.

"All right, let's go before you do actually pee your pants."

Benji stumbles a little as I lead him up the

stairs.

"Oh shit," he mutters and then giggles.

"Do *not* fall. If I have to catch you it's going to fuck up my shoulder," I warn.

"Psh, if anything around here is getting fucked, it's me."

"What?" I gasp and laugh.

"What?" Benji repeats, full of innocence and flirtation.

"You, Benjamin, are trouble."

"Gag. Don't call me *Benjamin*. I'm not a founding father."

"Well, you're not a shaggy dog either, but you don't mind Benji," I tease.

"Oh my god, I *loved* that movie as a kid."

We both laugh again, finally reaching my floor. I get my door open, and Benji bolts past me to the bathroom. I kick off my shoes and toss my keys on the little table next to my door and then head into the kitchen to get some water. I realize as I pour myself a glass that I hadn't thought about my ex at all tonight. Obviously, I'm breaking my streak now, but I'm still going to count this as a win.

As if summoned by my mere thoughts, my phone starts to ring, and Elliot's name is displayed on the screen. I consider sending him to voicemail, but I'm drunk enough and pissed enough to decide that answering it is the better choice.

"What the fuck do you want?" I spit the

question as soon as I answer.

"I heard that Malcolm called you, and I wanted to explain."

"You were fucking someone else while we were still together, not much to explain."

"It's not what you think," he defends.

The door to the bathroom opens, and Benji stumbles out.

"Pear Bear, I..." he trails off, realizing I'm on the phone, giving me an apologetic look, and instead helps himself to a glass of water from my sink.

"Whatever, things are over between us anyway. It's not like it matters now," I say to Elliot, and the way Benji's eyes go wide, I know he's eavesdropping.

He's quiet on the other end, and I'm happy to take my small victory.

"We always had something special. I hate thinking the door is closed in the future because of a misunderstanding."

My jaw ticks, and I ball my fist up. Benji studies me, the wheels in his head clearly turning before he leans close and purrs into my ear loudly enough for Elliot to hear, "Are you coming back to bed, baby?"

"You aren't alone?" Elliot asks, the jealousy clear in his voice.

"Nope."

"Who's there? Are you seeing someone?"

"Benji Casparian," I answer, my eyes flick-

ing to Benji's to make sure he's okay with me saying it's him. He smiles and nods encouragingly,
his chin resting on my shoulder as he openly listens in on the conversation now.

"Benji...wait, the keyboardist for Downward Spiral?" Elliot asks, a hint of jealousy in his
voice.

"The one and only."

"How did you even...That's, um..."

"I've gotta go, El," I say, hanging up the
phone before he can say anything else.

"Sorry, did I overstep?" Benji asks me as
soon as I set the phone down.

"Not at all, I appreciate it," I assure him as
he extracts himself from me.

"Glad to help then. I know it seemed weird
when Donnie suggested it, but if you want help,
I'm happy to give it. That guy seems like a
douche."

I laugh even as sadness washes over me.
"I didn't think he was that bad when we were
together. We had our problems, but I never
thought..."

Benji hugs me again. "Some people are
really good at faking it."

"Yeah," I agree. "Sorry. You should go; London's waiting on you."

"Are you sure? I can stay if you need someone to talk to."

"I appreciate it, but all I want is to get
some sleep."

"Okay, well, if you change your mind..." The wheels are turning in Benji's eyes again. "Honestly, it wouldn't exactly hurt my career to be seen around with you."

With that, Benji slips out quietly, and I drag myself to bed, stripping out of my clothes and climbing beneath the sheets, wondering what might have happened like if I'd told Benji to stay.

TRACK 10: SIDE B

Dreaming

Benji

London snored quietly in his bed while I tossed and turned on the floor beside it. He offered to let me share, but he tended to kick in his sleep, so the floor was a much safer bet. I wasn't sure why, but I'd been restless lately. We were sixteen and had only recently gotten our drivers licenses, and my new favorite past time was getting into my beat-up little Toyota, crank up the music, and just drive. I was counting down the days until graduation, which was still over two years away.

My phone made a skittering sound as it vibrated on the floor beside me. I reached for it, already expecting it to be a text from Lincoln. The only other person who would possibly text me at midnight was sound asleep three feet away from me.

Lincoln: You up?
Benji: Yup
Lincoln: Can you get out?

I smirked as I typed back in the affirmative. This was one of the things I loved about Lincoln; he might be a bit moody at times, but he was completely dedicated to making something happen with our band. It had become a fairly common occurrence to get messages from him in the middle of the night to tell us all to get our asses to whatever backwater bar he'd talked his way onto the makeshift stage of. And all of us were more than willing to climb out of our windows to do it.

I was wary when I first met Lincoln and Jude last year. Frankly, they were intimidating as fuck. They exuded an undeniable *fuck off* aura where most of the world was concerned, but for some reason they seemed to like me. Lando was a lot less intimidating, more laid back, but just as dedicated to the band as the rest of us were.

After I'd started casually talking to Lincoln and Jude on occasion in our shared study hall, I overheard them talking about starting a band, and I'd jumped at the chance to tell them I was proficient in a number of instruments *and* my parents had a garage they'd likely be willing to let us play in. That had been all they needed to hear to get excited by the prospect.

With London getting busy with all his different clubs and activities, I found myself eating lunch more and more often with Lincoln, Jude, and Lando, reading lyrics for songs

Lando and Lincoln wrote, and talking about our dreams of being a huge rock band, touring the world.

After getting another text from Lincoln about the bar where he was waiting for us, I slipped out of my makeshift bed and dressed quickly and quietly, not bothering to wake London. It wouldn't be the first time he woke up to find me gone to a gig, and I doubted it would be the last. It happened so often, I'd taken to keeping my keyboard in the trunk of my car, just in case.

I considered going through London's window, but he was on the second floor, and the last time I tried shimmying down the big tree, I'd shown up at the gig all scratched up and bleeding. So, I decided to risk tiptoeing through the house to go out the front door.

When I reached the first floor, I stopped in my tracks, holding my breath at the sound of the television coming from the living room. I peeked my head around the corner cautiously, relaxing when I spotted Paris rather than either of their parents.

"Hey, couldn't sleep?" he asked quietly.

"No, um, I'm actually sneaking out to go play at a bar a few towns over," I confessed, and Paris perked up.

"Yeah? That sounds fucking awesome."

My stomach fluttered. Over the past few years since I started hanging out over here, there had certainly been a bit of whiplash as far as the attention Paris paid to me. Sometimes he'd go weeks acting like I didn't exist, leaving the house any time I came to sleep over. Other times, we'd sit up late at night talking after London fell asleep. I craved his attention like oxygen, and it was embarrassing as hell.

"You want to come?" I offered, fully expecting him to decline the offer.

"Seriously? You wouldn't mind me tagging along?"

"Mind? You'll probably be the only sober person in the audience; it would be great."

"Do you have a minute for me to get dressed?" he asked, scrambling off the couch and gesturing at his pajama pants.

"Yeah, but hurry up, or Lincoln will throw a fit."

Paris sprinted to his bedroom with impressive stealth, returning less than a minute later in a pair of jeans, shoes already on.

"Holy shit, that was fast."

He shrugged. "Years of changing in the locker room as fast as possible," he explained.

We made it out of the house, sharing a conspiratorial smile as we climbed into my car.

"This is super lame, but this is the first time I've ever snuck out," he admitted as we pulled out of his driveway.

"I don't sneak out for parties or hookups or anything," I said with a shrug. "I sneak out for gigs a lot though."

"You're like a real rock star," he mused.

"I don't know about all that," I chuckled, feeling warm at the impressed tone of Paris' voice. "Maybe one day."

I was surprised to find we had a lot to talk about during our twenty-minute drive to the bar, from school to general adolescent complaints.

"I can't wait to get out of this town," I confided. "I think the band is my best bet to see the world like I want to, but if it doesn't work out, I'll figure something out."

"I have no doubt about that," Paris said with a warm laugh. "You're one of the most driven people I've ever met." His words, paired with the affection in his tone, startled me. I couldn't help but steal a glance at him before turning my attention back to the road just as the bar came into view.

Lincoln, Jude, and Lando were all waiting in the parking lot of the bar when I pulled up.

"Oh, hey, London," Jude greeted as we climbed out of my car.

"It's not—" I started to correct him, but Lincoln cut me off.

"Come on, we have to hurry up and get set up. Last call is in an hour, so we need to get our asses on that stage, or we won't have time to play."

"Can I help with anything?" Paris offered,

and the guys started pointing out amps and things he could grab, then we all hauled ass into the bar and set up our equipment at lightning speed.

Paris claimed a seat at a table close to the stage, looking up at us in awe as Lincoln introduced us, and Jude tapped out the countdown to start our first song.

My fingers flew over the keyboard without effort, having practiced these songs over and over until I could play them backward, forward, and in my sleep. Lincoln's smooth voice delivered the heartfelt lyrics while Jude and Lando set the beat. My own bias aside: we sounded fucking incredible. Maybe we weren't professional yet, but we were certainly a hell of a lot better than anyone expected out of a high school garage band.

My eyes met Paris' as I played, and there was a heat there I hadn't expected. It settled in my stomach and lit me up from the tips of my toes all the way to the top of my head. Unable to help myself, I shot him a flirty wink and, it was hard to tell in the dim light of the bar, but I swear he blushed.

We might have only been playing to a bar full of half-conscious drunks in Middle-Of-Nowhere, Ohio, but we played our hearts out as if we were playing to a packed arena full of screaming fans. We didn't stop until the bartender came over to wave at us, telling us it was last call, and we needed to pack up.

"You know, you guys aren't half bad," he said as we started getting our gear put away.

"Yeah?" Lincoln said with a bright smile. "How about letting us play a little earlier in the night next time? Say, ten o'clock next Saturday night?"

The bartender chuckled and nodded his head. "You're tenacious kid; I'll give you that."

"Is that a yes?" Lincoln pressed.

"Sure, what the hell. You bring that same fire next week, and I might even be able to talk the boss into paying you to entertain the customers after that."

"Thank you, sir," Lincoln said, reaching out to shake his hand.

"No problem. Your band have a name?" he asked.

"Downward Spiral," Jude said with a smirk. The name had been his brain child, and we all loved it. It was tempting fate and a little cheeky, exactly how we felt.

"You guys were amazing," Paris said, approaching the stage after the bartender left us to finish packing up.

"You think?" I fished, batting my eyelashes just a little.

"Can you flirt with your boyfriend later, Benj? I gotta get home before my dad realizes I'm gone," Lincoln complained.

"Psh, at least your dad would care. I'm just

going to walk right through my front door, slamming it on my way in, and I guarantee my dad won't even notice," Jude griped.

"Yeah, my dad will fucking care. He might just care enough to smash another guitar, which would mean I won't be able to play until I can find a way to buy a new one," Lincoln pointed out darkly.

"Sorry," Jude muttered while Lando and I shifted uncomfortably, eyes downcast. Neither of us understood the relationships Lincoln or Jude had with their parents, so we tried to stay quiet when the subject came up.

We finished cleaning up in a quiet hurry and then all returned to our cars to head home.

"Thanks so much for inviting me. This was so cool," Paris said as we drove away. "You guys are going to be huge; I can feel it."

TRACK 11: SIDE A

One Bed

Benji

The snow is falling outside, turning this small town into an almost picturesque snow globe. Inside London's small apartment, the smell of pizza from the open boxes on the coffee table fills the air, and the sound of London, Paris, and me jeering and cursing each other bounces off the walls, no doubt driving his neighbors crazy. It's like being transported back to being fifteen, the three of us playing video games and eating greasy pizza, except now there's also beer.

As the race finishes with me in second place and Paris in fourth, my phone vibrates in my pocket. I pull it out and see Lincoln's name lighting up the screen.

"Hello?" I answer, stifling a laugh as London and Paris fight over the last piece of pizza.

"Hey, Benny," he says in a soft voice, and my heart stills before jumping into my throat.

"Lincoln, how're you doing?" I ask cautiously, my hands shaking as I silently pray this isn't some sort of suicide call. Is it possible he's lying on the floor of his cabin right now bleeding out and calling me to say goodbye or something fucked up like that?

"I'm good. Great, actually. Archer was right. This vacation was just what the doctor ordered," he says, sounding suspiciously chipper. The sound of his guitar strumming in the background calms my heart rate down to almost normal. He wouldn't be playing his guitar while he's bleeding out, right? "You should see the snow here. It's so pristine, not like the gray snow on the sidewalks in New York. The stars too, there's so many of them. I'm so glad I came here, it's so pure and perfect." He races through the words, nearly stumbling over them, he's talking so fast.

"Slow down, man. You're going a mile a minute, and are you actually playing your guitar? How long has it been since you've picked it up off-stage?"

"Ages. It feels good. *I* feel good."

I twirl a finger through my hair, biting my lip as I press the phone harder to my ear. Drugs have never been Lincoln's thing as far as I know, but he sure sounds high as fuck right now.

"What's going on, Lincoln?"

"What do mean? I feel good for a change, so something must be *going on*?" he snaps defensively.

"I didn't mean it like that. This isn't like you, that's all. Is this like those times when you don't sleep for a week, calling in the middle of the night with ideas for drum solos and shit, and then you crash hard when it's all over?"

"Fuck you, I don't do that," he argues, clearly growing more agitated by the second.

"Linc," I sigh. "I'm worried about you, up at that cabin all alone."

"But I'm not alone," he says. "Jace is here."

Fucking fuck. Either Lincoln is having some sort of mental break—drug induced or otherwise—or the ex he nearly killed himself over is actually there. I'm not sure which of those two possibilities is worse.

"Jace is there?" I ask cautiously. "You haven't taken any drugs or anything, have you?"

"No," he snaps. "It's not an hallucination, asshole. Jace is here, next door. He's staying at his family cabin through Christmas. We've been talking and hanging out a little bit. I think... I think I might have a chance to make things right."

"And if you can't make things right?" I ask, terrified at the prospect. "What happens if you lose him all over again? I don't think you can survive that."

"No, I don't expect I can," he agrees somberly, doing nothing to make me feel any better about the situation.

"Listen—"

"I have to get going. I'll talk to you later." he cuts me off and hangs up before I can finish talking. I stare at the phone in my hand, unsure if I should call him back or not.

I take a deep breath and close my eyes, trying to decide what I need to do.

"Everything okay?" London asks, his laughter now morphed into concern.

"I'm not sure. That was Lincoln, and he sounded really weird."

"How weird? Like, do you need to call him an ambulance?"

"I don't think so. I'm just not really sure what to do," I admit. I've never been very good at managing Lincoln, or Jude for that matter. Letting Lando and Archer handle those two has been my go-to move, and as much as I wish I knew what to do about this on my own, I'm too worried about the situation to make this decision.

I pull Lando up in my contacts and dial him.

"Hey," Lando answers, sounding distracted and upset.

"Uh…hey," I reply. Shit, maybe I shouldn't have called him to lay this shit on him. It's not like Lando hasn't already done his fair share of babysitting Lincoln over the years. "Are you okay?"

"Fucking peachy, what's up?" he bites out uncharacteristically. I'm tempted to tell him never mind and let him go, but my worry for our lead singer has me powering forward.

"I just got a weird call from Lincoln."

"Is he okay?" His tone softens, the irritation being replaced with worry.

"I'm not sure, honestly. He called me Benny, and he was talking about a mile a minute. I think he's having one of his episodes where he doesn't sleep."

"Fucking hell," Lando sighs, and I hear the rustle of sheets.

"I'm really worried about him," I continue. "He said Jace is there." The words hang in the air for a few moments before Lando lets out a curse.

"*Jace*?" he repeats in horror.

"Yeah," I confirm, feeling about the same way he sounds. "I can't decide if this is good news or not. If they work things out, maybe Lincoln will finally get help. But if things go south...I don't think he'll survive it."

"Agreed," he says grimly.

"Maybe I should call Archer? I hate to bother him when he deserves a vacation so much too."

"Why don't we give Lincoln a few days, and then I'll call him to check in?"

"Okay, yeah," I agree, glad to have the decision taken out of my hands. "How's your vacation going?" I ask conversationally.

He makes a sound that's difficult to interpret and then turns the conversation around. "You?"

"It's *interesting.*"

"Oh yeah? You and London rekindling the old flame?" Lando guesses. I can hear his suggestive grin through the phone.

"How many times do I have to tell you guys that London and I aren't *together*? I feel like I should take out a billboard or something. And, no, we're not casually fooling around again or anything else," I say casting a glance over at London and Paris who are no longer interested in my conversation, instead focused on the video game, London having claimed my controller to kick his brother's ass in *Mario Kart.* "Oh? Who's keeping you so *interested*?" Lando teases.

"No one yet, but we'll see how things go." I eye Paris. Even knowing my rekindling crush won't ever amount to anything, it's hard not to enjoy the time we're getting to spend together on this visit. He glances over at me, and our eyes linger on each other for a few seconds, a strange sort of electricity flowing between us until London cheers, and Paris tears his gaze away to see he's driven his car off the road in the game.

"You have your eye on someone in particular?"

"I do. Not sure if I'm going to be able to pull it off. We'll see," I laugh. It's all bluster; I have no shot with Paris, but it's fun to pretend.

"If you're gunning for the guy, he doesn't stand a chance."

"Aw, thanks, boo."

"Any time, sugar plum," he jokes back.

We chat for a few more minutes before both signing off.

Without warning, I reach over and snatch the controller out of London's hand, causing the Bowser on the screen to go over the edge of the track and London to shout in protest.

Paris chuckles at his brother's outrage and sails over the finish line in first place.

"Mother fucker, I was going to beat him," London complains.

"Suck it up, it's my turn."

Paris

"Shit, that's a lot of snow," I say, looking out the window and stretching my arms after our long gaming marathon. I wince at the familiar ache in my shoulder, being careful not to stretch it too hard.

"You guys should crash here," London suggests. "The roads probably aren't plowed yet."

One of the many downsides of this tiny ass town is that there's *one* plow guy, and he refuses to go out late at night, plowing only the main road through town and leaving everything else until the morning.

"Cool, I call your bed," Benji declares with a smirk.

My stomach twists with a hint of jealousy at the thought of them fooling around while

I sleep on the couch. I heard Benji tell Lando that he and London aren't together, but it's hard to shake the memory of seeing them fooling around back in high school.

"You can have my bed, but you're sharing it with Paris, not me," London counters.

My eyebrows go up, and Benji fixes London with a chiding look I don't understand.

"Is that so?" Benji says in a bored sort of voice.

"Yeah, the couch is too hard on his bad shoulder," he explains reasonably. He's not wrong, but why am I getting the strange feeling there's subtext here I'm not privy to?

"It'll be fine," I assure London. "One night on the couch won't kill me."

"Bullshit," he says. "You're only a few months away from training camp, and your shoulder is still bugging you. I'm not going to have you suing me for ruining your career by making you sleep on my couch."

"Don't worry, 'Ris, I can keep my hands to myself," Benji jokes.

Too bad, I think and then scold myself for thinking of Benji that way. I know I'm fighting a losing battle against my thoughts, but I still need to try.

With the matter seemingly settled, London goes into his bedroom to grab one of the many pillows off his bed and brings it to the couch.

"Go to bed," he says, making a shooing motion at us before he pulls his throw blanket off the back of the couch and over himself.

Benji and I head down the hallway to London's bedroom, the air between us feeling awkward and heavy. I make a pitstop in the bathroom on our way down the hallway, hoping it'll be less weird if I give Benji a few minutes to get out of his jeans and climb into bed before I get there. Splashing some water on my face, I grab a spare toothbrush from under the sink and brush my teeth, then I take a piss, and finally make my way to the bedroom.

The room is dark, and it takes my eyes a second to adjust. There's more light from the moon than usual thanks to the reflection off the snow, so once my eyes are used to it, I can see easily.

Benji's lying on his side, facing toward the window, his long hair fanned out over the pillow behind him. He turns his head to look over his shoulder at me with a half-smile on his lips.

"Come on, I don't bite," he encourages, and heat flares in the pit of my stomach.

Maybe if I hadn't been such a chickenshit when we were younger about my sexuality, if I'd embraced it like London did, I could've had Benji instead. It feels like such a betrayal to my brother to even think it, but I can't think of anything I've wanted more in my life than Benji.

In the dark of the bedroom, a warm co-

coon as snow falls heavy outside, and Benji smiling at me in that way, it's too easy to pretend for a few seconds that he *is* mine. I can convince myself that I'm about to climb into bed next to him and have the freedom to kiss and touch him.

Before I can let my fantasy get the better of me, I hastily strip out of my jeans and pull back the covers to climb into bed. I shiver as the cool sheets wrap around me.

"Jeez, you could've at least rolled around a bit to warm the bed up before I got in," I complain playfully.

"Oh sorry, I'm used to warming up a bed in much more interesting ways," he teases back, and I bite my tongue against suggesting we do just that.

My mind keeps going back to Benji's words when he was on the phone earlier—*we aren't together*. Did he mean him and London? Was he talking about someone else? Not that it matters. Obviously, he's not with London anymore now, but they *were* together, and that's enough to make me a horrible brother for even entertaining the thought.

Silence falls between us, and even though it's obvious neither of us are sleeping, I think talking in bed feels way too intimate, so we both lay quietly until we fall asleep.

*****

Hair tickles my nose, bringing with it the expensive smell of a hair salon. A warm, slim body fills my arms, the curve of an ass cradling my morning erection. Still half-asleep and almost ninety percent sure this is a fantastic dream, I tighten my grip and twitch my hips, dragging my cock against the person sleeping pressed against me.

"Mmm," he hums happily, and my eyes fly open.

Oh fuck, I just dry humped my brother's ex-boyfriend. I scramble out of the bed, probably setting a land speed record as I put as much space between us as possible.

"What the fuck?" Benji grumbles, rolling over and looking around, his eyes clouded with sleep and confusion.

My heart is thundering as I stand next to the bed, using a pillow to cover my erection, unable to stop looking at Benji, my body craving everything about him. His hair is all mussed, sleep lines indenting his cheek, his tongue darting out to moisten his dry lips. It's all I can do not to crawl back in bed beside him and find out if his mouth tastes the same as I remember.

He sits up and rubs his eyes, yawning loudly and stretching his arms over his head.

"Fuck, I hate sleeping with my contacts in, my eyes are dry as fuck now."

"I...um," I clear my throat, torn between

bolting for the door and climbing back into bed. My head and body can't seem to get on the same page about what the best course of action is, both of them calling me a fucking idiot for just standing there with a pillow pressed against my still hard dick.

"I need to piss," Benji says, throwing back the blankets and climbing out of bed. I watch him as he saunters half-naked out of the room without a care in the world, his hair flowing behind him like he's a runway model. And I swear you'd never know I'm a rich, charismatic man who never has trouble getting a man's attention by the way I stare after him until he's long since left the room.

"Fuck my life," I mutter to myself, flinging the pillow back onto the bed and getting dressed.

I find London still fast asleep on the couch. I hastily jot a note telling him I'll see him at Mom and Dad's for Christmas in a few days, and hurry to put my shoes and coat on, fleeing the apartment before Benji finishes in the bathroom.

I know it's a lame as fuck move, running out of there like my ass is on fire, but if I don't get away from Benji, I'm afraid I'm going to do something really fucking stupid like kiss him or tell him I've had a hopeless crush on him half my life.

As I get into my car and start the drive home on the still snowy roads, I can't stop thinking about the feeling of Benji in my arms, the smell of his hair surrounding me, the sound of his sleep rough voice. As if I needed more things to dream about when it comes to Benji.

TRACK 12: SIDE B

What if I Am?

Paris

The guys were acting wild. It always happened after a win, everyone in the locker room wrestling, snapping towels, and talking shit. I couldn't believe this would be my last year with this group of guys who had become like brothers to me. We were seniors, and next year we'd all be going to different schools. Not just me and my teammates, but I probably would be away from my brother for the first time...and Benji.

The thought of not seeing Benji every day hurt like hell. I tried to keep my distance from him, but even so, he was always *there*—at my school, in my house...in my dreams every damn night.

"If you did him from behind, you could pretend he's a girl," one of the guys joked loudly, his voice booming over all the ruckus, my body tensing at his words. I already knew who he was talking about without having to hear the full statement.

"Fucking fag," someone else shouted at

him jokingly.

"It's not gay if you're the one giving it," the first guy argued. "I bet I could make that little homo squeal."

My jaw ticked, and my hands balled into fists. "Shut the fuck up," I shouted without thinking.

An eerie silence fell over the locker room, and I turned to face the person who had been talking all the shit—Tribskie.

"What, am I insulting your boyfriend?" he mocked, and a nervous laugh went through the room.

"Don't be an idiot," I grumbled, anxiety rising in the pit of my stomach.

"Do you *looooove* him?" Tribskie continued to taunt. "You want to hold him and kiss him?"

With two strides, I crossed the space between us, shoving the mouthy fucker up against his locker.

"Shut the fuck up."

He didn't look scared as I held him against the locker, my fists balling the front of his shirt. If anything, he looked calculating, and that scared the shit out of *me*.

"Are you a faggot, Jones?" he asked point blank and for some reason, I was sick and tired of lying.

"Yeah, Trib, I am." I released him and took a step back, turning to face the rest of the team.

"Anyone have a problem with that?"

Most of the guys dropped their gaze to their feet, clearly uncomfortable but not sure what to say to the team captain and quarterback coming out unexpectedly.

When no one said anything, I stalked back over to my own locker and finished getting dressed.

I felt everyone's eyes on me the entire time, but I kept my head high and didn't let them see me sweat. Once I was dressed, I casually walked out of the locker room without a backward glance while my heart pounded a tattoo against my ribs.

Benji

Everyone at school was whispering gossip, and for the first time in my seventeen years of life, I wasn't the topic of conversation.

"Do you think it's true?" London whispered to me as we made our way to third period.

"How should I know? He's your brother. Have you seen him with gay porn or anything?"

"I don't know; I don't go snooping through his stuff."

I shrugged. "It might be true. I mean, he *never* dates," I pointed out in an even voice, my heart beating hard and fast. Stupid heart, even if Paris was gay, that didn't mean he was into me like I was him.

"Maybe we should..." Whatever London

was about to suggest trailed off when we spotted Paris slipping out the side door at the end of the hallway. I'm not sure why they didn't stick a teacher near that door because everyone knew it was the best door to use when you wanted to ditch out in the middle of the day without getting caught.

"Should we go after him?" I asked.

"Yeah, let's go."

We hurried down the hall and did a quick check around to make sure there weren't any teachers nearby before pushing through the doors and stepping out into the back parking lot.

"Paris!" London called as we jogged to catch up with the retreating form of his brother, already halfway across the parking lot. His steps faltered, and he glanced over his shoulder at us.

"Go back to class," Paris said as soon as we caught up to him.

"Why are you taking off? Is it because of what everyone's saying?" London asked.

Paris scoffed but didn't deny it, his eyes fixed on his shoes and his shoulders slumped.

"Paris," I said his name gently, reaching out to touch his arm. "*Are* you gay?"

He looked up, his light green eyes dancing with equal parts anxiety and determination. "Yeah, I am."

A slow smile spread across my face, and I looked over at London to see the same. We both stepped forward, surrounding Paris and hugging him tightly.

"Welcome to the club, bro," London said with a laugh.

"We'll make sure you get signed up for orientation as soon as possible," I joked, and they both laughed.

"You think Mom and Dad will be disappointed they have *two* gay sons?" he asked.

"No way," London assured him.

"Well, I *know* the NFL isn't going to be very accepting of a gay quarterback, so even if it feels like a huge weight is off right now, I'm going to have to sneak back into the closet when I go to college."

"Let's not think about that right now," I suggested. "Today's a big day; let's go do something to celebrate."

"Yeah?" Paris asked hopefully. "Like what?"

"We'll think of something."

TRACK 13: SIDE A

Ghost of Christmas Past
Benji

Waking up Christmas morning in my old bedroom, in my lumpy twin bed, makes me happier than I could've imagined. I stretch and groan, the smell of pancakes reaching my nose and making my stomach growl.

I grab my phone and shoot a quick Merry Christmas text to London. He invited me to his family Christmas dinner tonight, which I happily accepted. It was a tradition when we were teenagers that I'd spend Christmas Eve and Christmas morning with my parents and then go for their family dinner. I've been dreaming of his mom's chicken and dumplings since I found out I'd be home for Christmas.

Throwing back my blankets, I climb out of bed and shiver. Glancing around my room, I notice one of my old hoodies still neatly folded on top of my dresser. I get up and put it on, suddenly feeling seventeen all over again in a Panic! At the Disco hoodie. It's not a bad feeling.

Trotting down the stairs, I find my parents in the kitchen—my mom making breakfast while my dad drinks coffee and reads the newspaper at the kitchen table. It feels familiar and comforting, and it's the best possible Christmas present I could ask for.

I can still remember our first Christmas away on tour. Lincoln was particularly sullen, I assume missing Jace, and Jude was on a coke binge. Lando and I holed up in his hotel room and did our best to pretend we weren't homesick. We both called our parents and acted like we didn't notice the other shedding a few tears as we ate crappy room service burgers and missed our moms like five-year-olds on their first day of kindergarten.

"Sit, I got your favorite syrup," my mom says proudly when she notices me entering the kitchen.

"That boysenberry one?" I guess.

"That's the one."

Growing up, we only got the fancy, fruity syrup on Christmas because it was too expensive to buy the rest of the year. I could afford to buy an entire boysenberry farm and have my own syrup bottled now, but I still save it solely for Christmas.

"Are you going to London's house for dinner?" she asks, and I snort a laugh. It really does sound like we're teenagers again.

"Yes, his mom invited me for dinner like usual."

"Good. I'm so glad you and London stayed close after you left to travel the world."

"Me too."

"He's such a nice boy," she goes on. "Handsome too."

"Oh, for fuck sake," I groan. "Not you too."

"What?"

"I'm *not* dating London. We've never dated." I leave out the fact that we used to fool around because I am *so* not telling my mother that.

"I hate seeing you so lonely."

"I'm not lonely," I lie. "I have tons of friends."

"Psh, those aren't friends."

I bristle, the comment hitting too close to home. "I have friends," I argue again. "I'm friends with Cooper, and when we were in Vegas a little while ago, I made friends with this kick ass tattoo artist who I still message with."

"Well, that's nice," she says but doesn't sound convinced.

"The pancakes smell good," I say, changing the subject before the shitty feeling her words are creating can grow any bigger. The reminder of how it feels to be the kid all alone on the playground, the kid with no one at his birthday party, the kid always eating by himself in the lunchroom, is too much to bear, especially on Christmas morning.

Mercifully, the subject is dropped and

we're able to spend the rest of the morning doing Christmas right—eating pancakes, drinking hot cocoa, exchanging presents that my parents insist I spent too much money on, and watching Christmas movies.

With my mother's words about me not having any real friends other than London still weighing on my mind though, halfway through *A Christmas Story*, I pull out my phone and shoot Merry Christmas texts to both Royal, the tattoo artist I met when we were in Las Vegas, and Cooper.

Royal: You too! Hope you're having a good holiday. Are you somewhere insanely awesome?

Benji: Do you consider my parents living room in Ohio insanely awesome? Lol

Royal: If it's where you want to be on Christmas, then hell yeah.

I glance over at my mom and dad, sharing a blanket, engrossed in the movie, and I smile.

Benji: Yeah, it's where I want to be.

Royal: Glad to hear it.

Benji: You spending the holiday surrounded by family?

Royal: Spent the morning with my brother and my men, and tonight we're having a big family dinner with all the guys from the shop. It's the perfect Christmas

Jealousy blooms in my stomach. Don't get me wrong; I love my parents to death, but it must be incredible to have a family of his own with his boyfriends.

Benji: That's awesome! When I get back to New York, I'm going to fly you out to do some new ink for me.
Royal: Can't wait.

See? I have friends. Cooper's response is a lot briefer simply saying Merry Christmas and that we should get together when we're both back in the city. He hints at being somewhere interesting for Christmas, and I tell him with a tease like that he can bet I'll be tracking him down soon to get the details.

When the morning slowly becomes the afternoon, I drag myself off the couch to take a shower and get dressed for the Christmas party at the Jones'. Aside from the tradition of chicken and dumplings, ugly Christmas sweaters are part of the required dress code. I pull on my red and green sweater featuring a Rudolph, complete with light up nose and garlands attached to the sweater around his antlers. I take the time to blow-dry my hair and then place a pair of sequin antlers on top of my head and declare myself ready to go.

Paris

The traditional Bing Crosby Christmas album is playing from my dad's record player, the smell of chicken and dumplings, pine, and hot apple cider fill the air, and snow is just starting to fall outside. It's an idyllic Christmas scene if I've ever seen one.

I've missed so many Christmases at home since signing with the team out in LA. I didn't realize until this moment how much it hasn't felt like Christmas all these years. Going to some snooty party just wasn't the same as a family Christmas.

The front door opens, and Benji steps in wearing a pair of gaudy antlers atop his head without shame. His whole face lights with a big smile as the family greets him. My mom gives him a big hug and tells him he needs a haircut.

"You and my mom are ganging up on me," he complains good-naturedly, giving my dad a hug next, and then kissing London on the cheek and wishing him a Merry Christmas.

Then his gaze lands on me, and I smile. There's something about Benji's attention that has a way of making you feel like the most important person in the world. It's not just that he's rich and famous either. I've been around plenty of celebrities, and very few of them have that particular super power that Benji has effortlessly perfected.

He walks over to me until he's fully in my personal space, tilting his head back slightly so he can look at me. He leans up and presses his lips to my cheek, warming me from head to toe.

When he pulls back, he grins at me and points up. "Mistletoe."

I tilt my head up to see the decoration above my head, feeling a hint of disappointment that the kiss wasn't spontaneous.

"Right."

He turns back to my mom and turns on his most charming smile. "What do I have to do to get some of that apple cider that smells so good?"

"Help yourself; it's in the slow cooker in the kitchen."

Benji and London disappear into the kitchen together, and I stand there watching him go, wondering what the fuck is wrong with me that even after all this time I can't stop crushing on my brother's man this hard.

My parents make small talk with Benji for a while, listening raptly as he regales them with tales of his travels, his vast collection of art and culture, his famous friends, and on and on. But as he talks I notice something: there's a strange sort tightness around his eyes, a slight desperation in his tone, and I wonder if he's trying this hard to impress himself rather than anyone else.

When dinner is ready, we're all ushered into the dining room, and I end up sitting between Benji and London.

"So, Paris, how's your shoulder healing? Think you'll be back next season as planned?" my dad asks once we're all seated, plates piled high with delicious food.

I know he's trying to be supportive, but I'd have preferred if he'd punched me in the stomach rather than bring up the subject of my injury.

"I'm not sure yet," I lie.

"It'll be okay," my mom says reassuringly. "If you leave the NFL, things will still work out."

Leave the NFL, as if it's a choice I have to make. I've lived and breathed football as long as I can remember, and in the space between two breaths, I lost it all. What am I supposed to do with myself now? I don't even know who I am anymore.

At least when I was in LA with Elliot there was plenty to distract me, to keep me from wallowing. But now what?

"There's still plenty of time for me to keep working on rehab," I say, not sure if I'm trying to convince them or myself.

I catch a sympathetic look on Benji's face, and I hate it a little. I don't need sympathy. What happened, happened.

After dinner, everyone piles into the living room to watch *Rudolph*, but I grab a glass of hot cider and slip out onto the back sun-porch to watch the snow fall for a few minutes and clear my head.

When the door behind me creaks open, I'm not sure if I'm surprised or not to see it's Benji who followed me out here.

"You okay?" he asks gently, easing down into one of the wicker chairs beside me. I shrug and take a sip of my drink, letting it warm me up a little. "I'm pretty sure the band is breaking up," he confesses when I don't say anything. "And I am fucking *terrified.*"

"It sucks when you pour your entire life into something and then it goes away in the blink of an eye," I say.

"God, it *seriously* sucks," he agrees emphatically. "Fuck is it cold out here," he complains with a laugh, wrapping his arms around himself.

"I'm fine; you don't need to sit out here and babysit me or anything," I assure him.

"The snow is pretty," he says, turning his attention to the snowflakes coming down. "In New York the snow is such a pain in the ass. Here it's kind of nice."

"Yeah, I always hated the snow, but I think I've missed it since moving out to California."

A comfortable silence falls between us, both of us enjoying the quiet and our warm drinks until it becomes too cold to bear any longer, and we go back inside to join my family in the living room. When Benji plops down on the couch next to London, the jealousy in the pit of my stomach feels even stronger than usual, and I hate myself for it.

TRACK 14: SIDE A

Escape

Benji

"I'm bored," I say as soon as London swings open the door to his apartment.

It's been two days since Christmas, and as much as I've enjoyed spending time with my parents, I feel like I'm going a little stir crazy already after ten days in Ohio.

"That was quick, even for you." He waves me in, and I follow him to his living room, plopping myself down on the couch and putting my feet up on his scuffed-up coffee table, covered in ring shaped stains from a thousand different drinks over the years.

"I don't understand it. When I'm not here it's all I can think about, but then once I come home it starts to feel...itchy."

"You know what they say: you can't go home again."

I sigh and wrap a strand of hair around my index finger, twirling and untwirling it while I think.

"Let's go to the beach."

London raises his eyebrows at me. "It's December, and we're in Ohio."

"No, I mean let's get the hell out of here. I have this buddy who owns a little strip of beach on some remote Caribbean Island. He owes me a favor. I'll call and ask if we can borrow it for a week," I suggest. "We can lay out in the sand, drinking and soaking up the sun. We can swim with sea turtles and go hiking to find hidden waterfalls; it'll be amazing." The idea sounds better and better to me the more I pitch it, a flutter of excitement starting in my chest. London, however, looks skeptical.

"I have a lot of work to do. I can't just fuck off on some last-minute vacation and leave my clients hanging."

"Come on, Donnie." I stick out my bottom lip in an exaggerated pout. "We'll fly out on a private jet and everything."

"I'm sorry, B, I don't think so."

Now that the idea has fully formed in my head, I don't want to let it go. It sounds like heaven, and I'm going with or without London.

"Fine, I guess I'll go alone," I sigh and shoot him a pathetic look, one last attempt to change his mind.

"Why don't you take Paris? God knows he could use a vacation."

My stomach does a somersault, my pulse speeding up at the thought of just me and Paris, all alone on a private beach, drinking and walking around half-naked to cope with the heat. My cock starts to harden at the thought.

"He won't want to go," I reason. Sure, we've been spending some time together in the past ten days, but every time we're together, he seems so tense, like he's just waiting to get the hell away from me.

London shrugs. "Doesn't hurt to ask."

I chew on my bottom lip and flip my hair back and forth absently as I consider the suggestion.

"Can I have his number?" I ask after a few seconds, pulling out my phone so I can dial as he recites it.

It rings two times, three, four, and I'm about to hang up when he finally answers.

"Hello?"

"Hey, 'Ris, it's Benji."

"Oh, hey," he sounds confused but not *un*happy to hear it's me.

"Your brother gave me your number," I explain.

"Oookay."

"This is going to sound incredibly weird, but how would you like to take a private jet to a secluded island and spend a week with me?"

"What?"

"Which part was confusing?" I tease.

"The part where you're inviting *me* on some crazy, rich person vacation."

"Well, Donnie turned me down, so you

were my backup."

"That makes only slightly more sense," he admits. "You must have a thousand friends who would love to spend a week on an island with you."

I chew on my bottom lip again. Sure, there are a lot of people I could ask, and I'm sure most of them would jump at the chance, but I'd much rather have Paris than any of my rich, impressive *friends*. Aside from my parents and London, Paris is probably the only other person in the world I can even kind of be myself around. The thought of spending an entire week being *on* for someone sounds exhausting. For the first time in my life, I don't want to be Rock Star Benji; I just want to be Benji.

"I'd rather spend a week relaxing with my oldest friend," I confess the closest thing to the truth I can manage.

"I thought London was your oldest friend," he jokes.

"Technically, I met you first."

"That's right, you did," he agrees in a slightly wistful tone before going quiet for a few seconds. "You know what? Fuck it, I'll come."

"You will?"

"Sure, why the hell not? It's not like I have anything to do around here other than sit around feeling sorry for myself," he reasons. "And I can do my exercises anywhere."

"I'll make the arrangements and let you

know. I'm sure we can leave in a few hours if that works for you?"

"Yeah, that'll work."

Paris

I'm half expecting a second call from either Benji or London telling me the whole thing is a practical joke. I consider several times calling him up to back out. This is crazy. A week ago I was running from London's apartment like it was on fire to get away from the temptation that is Benji. Now I'm going to spend an entire week on an island with him?

I pull out my of late little-used suitcase and start filling it with clothes—shorts, shirts with cut-off sleeves, underwear. Then, I start in on toiletries— toothbrush, soap, sunscreen that may or may not be expired at this point. When my hand inadvertently knocks an unopened bottle of lube onto the counter from the medicine cabinet, I pick it up and pause. Should I take some, just in case?

My stomach flutters at the thought of pretty little Benji riding me, head thrown back, cock bobbing freely with each swivel of his hips as he pleasures himself with my cock buried deep in his ass.

Groaning, I reach into my pants and adjust my rapidly growing erection. It's so fucking wrong to think of my brother's ex-boyfriend that way, and there is absolutely no doubt I'm going to hell for it. But still, I throw the bottle of lube and a nearly full box of condoms into my suitcase anyway. Call it wishful thinking, or tempting fate, or maybe just plain stupid.

There's a knock at my door, so I quickly zip my suitcase and go to answer it. Benji's standing in the hallway of my grungy apartment building looking as out of place as anyone ever has wearing a pair of sunglasses that probably cost more than a month of rent on their own, not to mention the rest of his designer label outfit, his hair sleek and soft looking as it cascades off his shoulders. The smile on his pretty pink lips has my dick interested all over again.

"All set to go?" he checks.

"Yup." I slip on my shoes and coat, pick up my suitcase, and glance back into my apartment to make sure I didn't leave any lights on or any-thing. Then, I step out into the hallway.

Before I can finish shutting my door, an-other set of footsteps echoes through the hall-way. I glance over my shoulder and freeze when I see Elliot coming up the stairs.

"Hey," I say awkwardly, and Benji whips his head around to see who's joining us.

Elliot's shoulders are tense as his eyes land on my suitcase.

"Going away for the weekend?" he guesses.

Benji puts on a smitten, indulgent smile, looking over at me like he's completely in love with me.

"A whole week actually," Benji says. "I'm selfishly whisking him away to this secluded little island in the Caribbean where we can ring in the new year naked on the beach. I want him all to myself for a full week of living off coconuts, rum, and orgasms."

My cock jerks at the filthy purr in his voice and the way he's looking at me like he might jump me right here in the hallway in front of my ex-boyfriend. If his music career goes south, the man has a future in acting without a doubt.

Elliot's mouth open and closes like a fish, his eyes darting between me and Benji and then returning to me with a pleading look.

"We'd love to stay and chat, but I have a private jet waiting for us, so we have to be going."

I bite back a smug smile and follow Benji down the stairs, out to the car waiting for us by the curb.

"I think I love you right now," I tell him after putting my suitcase into the trunk next to his and sliding into the backseat.

"Being impressively rich and horny is just one of the services I offer," he jokes. "Are you okay seeing him like that? Has he showed up here before?"

"God no, when we were together, he would pitch an absolute fit any time I wanted to come home to Ohio for a holiday or a weekend. I'm not even sure how he got ahold of my address."

"It kind of seems like he's desperate to get you back."

"Psh," I snort. "He doesn't want me back. He just doesn't want anyone else playing with one of his toys. And he doesn't like the idea that I might be dating someone more famous than he is."

The ride to the nearest regional airport doesn't take long. It's not until we get there that I realize how crazy this is. I'm going to be riding on a *private jet* to a secluded island for vacation.

"This is so crazy," I mutter, shaking my head and smiling as we board the plane.

"It's not *my* jet if that helps. I borrowed it from a friend."

"The fact that you have friends with private jets is impressive in its own right," I point out.

A flicker of pride followed by sadness crosses his face.

"I'm really glad you're coming with me. We're going to have fun," he says after a few quiet seconds.

"I'm glad you invited me."

TRACK 15: SIDE A

Paradise

Benji

The flight takes eight hours, including our stop to refuel. Paris and I doze on and off for most of it. When the plane finally lands at our destination, I'm itching to feel the sand between my toes and let the ocean air chase away the cold in my bones that New York and Ohio has left me with.

"Holy shit," Paris says as we step off the plane in a tropical paradise. "I mean, I've been some incredible places, but damn."

I take a deep breath, filling my lungs with warm, salty air and smiling. "This is *exactly* what we needed," I declare. "Hold on, I need to take a quick selfie."

I pause and snap a few pictures with only slightly different expressions so I can pick which one looks best and then start walking again toward our ride.

We climb into the car waiting to take us to the house, and I upload the picture to Instagram.

"Should we have taken a picture together?

I'm sure it would get under Elliot's skin to see it, and the media would eat it up. They've spent weeks going on and on about Elliot and his new man. I bet they're *dying* to see some answering drama from you," I say. He winces, and I feel like a bit of an asshole for suggesting it. He hasn't made a single social media post since his injury. Maybe he doesn't want anyone knowing what he's up to.

He hesitates again, confirming my theory. "I haven't posted in a while."

"I know," I admit. "I kind of stalk your Insta and Twitter."

His eyes go wide, and then he laughs. "Why?"

I shrug, because telling him I have a massive crush on him would probably start this vacation off on an awkward foot. "Why'd you stop posting?"

"I couldn't take the haters," he says. "When I was playing, it was easy to brush them off. But after my injury, I just couldn't take being kicked while I was down. And I've been spending all my time focused on rehabbing my shoulder; posting selfies has been the last thing on my mind."

"That's understandable. Forget I even suggested it."

"No, you know what, let's do it. Maybe it's time I stop hiding under my rock."

"You're sure?"

"Yes," he says resolutely, pulling out his own phone and scooting closer to me so we can get a picture together.

I watch as he uploads it to Instagram, quickly typing up a vague but upbeat description to go with the picture, adds me, and then adds a dozen or so tags before sharing it. I do the same and then put my phone away. Rolling down the window of the car, the warm air ripples through my hair, and the house we're staying at coming into view not far ahead.

"There it is," I point out.

"Holy shit, are you serious?" Paris takes in the grand beach house with wide eyes. "It looks huge. It must've cost a fortune."

"Well, it's free for us, so let's enjoy it."

Paris

To call this place a beach house is like calling a Clydesdale a pony. I've rubbed elbows with a lot of rich and famous people over the years and been inside a *lot* of impressive houses, but this one wins hands down. It's spacious with high vaulted ceilings and gorgeous, polished wood floors. The back of the house has floor to ceiling glass windows and a door that opens onto a sprawling porch that leads directly onto the beach. I'm not even sure how many bedrooms there are; I stopped counting after ten. I might be a *tad* disappointed that Benji and I won't be forced to share a bed again.

"I called ahead to have the housekeeper stock up the kitchen before we got here so there should be plenty of food and booze," Benji says.

The sun is already starting to set, but after sleeping on the plane most of the day I'm wide awake.

"I see a grill on the back porch; how about steaks and tequila to pass this lovely evening?" I suggest.

"That sounds incredible. Let me just grab a quick shower, and I'll meet you out there."

As he struts away, my eyes fall to his round little ass, and I think for the millionth time about how I'm *so* going to hell. Taking this trip with him was probably a huge mistake, but I can't find it in myself to regret it.

I change out of my warm clothes I wore from Ohio and into a pair of swim shorts and a sleeveless shirt. My ugly scar is prominent on my right shoulder, and I drag my fingers over the rough skin for a moment, thinking about how quickly life can change.

Benji wasn't kidding when he said the kitchen was stocked. There's enough food in the refrigerator that we could hole up here for a month without a problem. I find some strip steaks and pull them out, along with some zucchini I figure I can grill up as well to make the meal more well-rounded. Then I snag a bottle of expensive tequila from the liquor cabinet and head outside.

By the time I have the grill fired up, Benji comes out, dressed similarly to me in a pair of shorts and a tank top. I'm certain his outfit cost a hell of a lot more than mine, and he looks incredible. His hair is pulled up in a messy bun, his long neck exposed. Normally, I *hate* the man-bun look, but Benji totally pulls it off.

"The grill still needs to heat up," I let him know as he slides down into one of the chaise lounges on the patio. Leaning back and smiling, he tilts his head back to look up into the darkening sky.

"I've got nowhere to be," he assures me.

I pick up the bottle of tequila and make myself comfortable on the second chair, directly beside his. Unscrewing the cap, I take a sip and pass it over to Benji before leaning back.

Out of curiosity, I pull out my phone and check my notifications. Unsurprisingly, my Instagram has completely blown up with likes and comments on the picture of me and Benji.

I click on it and start to read through some of the comments. A lot of them are asking what happened between me and Elliot, a ton saying how good Benji and I look together, some suggestive or lewd ones about what Benji and I must be doing together on vacation, and, of course, a few haters. But one thing that's largely absent is any questions or comments about my injury or whether I'll be returning to the NFL next season.

Benji wanted to know why I've stayed off

social media, and I wasn't lying about the haters. But, more than that, it's been a constant reminder of the uncertainty of my career. At first, I was too depressed to post, then as I got back into working out and trying to get my shoulder back into shape, any time I posted a gym selfie or tweeted about physical therapy, the unanswerable questions were endless. Then, Elliot and I broke up, and I certainly wasn't going to post anything about that. And before I knew it, *months* had gone by without a post.

This though? People being interested in my life rather than my injury is nice.

"People are going apeshit over that selfie," Benji says, practically reading my thoughts.

"Yeah," I agree, liking a few comments before closing the app and setting my phone down to take another drink from the tequila bottle. "Listen, I know I sort of jumped down London's throat about it, but…"

"You want to fake date me?" Benji guesses with a smirk, taking the bottle from me.

"Is that just too childish?" I ask, getting a certain amount of glee from the thought of Elliot's head exploding if the story of Benji and me dating overshadows his own media drama.

Benji bites his bottom lip, looking out into the darkening horizon for a few seconds.

"Cards on the table?" he asks, and I nod, waving him to go on and say whatever is on his mind. "I know I told you this at Christmas, but

Downward Spiral is almost guaranteed to break up. I know Archer thinks this little vacation is going to magically fix everything, but Jude and Lincoln's issues are too big, and Lando's heart isn't in this anymore. We're through; it's just a matter of time."

"I'm sorry." If anyone can empathize with dreams crumbling and careers ending, it's me. I reach for his hand to comfort him. His skin is warm and soft to the touch.

"Jude and Lincoln are constantly in the headlines because of all their bullshit. Being the good boy in the band might make the label happy, but it certainly hasn't made me a household name. When people talk about Downward Spiral, they talk about Lincoln, Jude, the hot one who plays bass, and the guy on the keyboards with the hair," he continues. "With Jude and Lincoln tucked away out of the spotlight for the next month or so, if I could find a way to get some attention, I'll at least have *some* hope of doing something else once the band falls apart. I need to make sure people know me so I can get some dumbass reality TV show or *something*."

I blow out a long breath. It's basically what Elliot wanted from me when we first met, except Benji is being a lot more upfront about it. Plus, this isn't some random famewhore who's trying to jump on my dick to get noticed; this is *Benji*. And I *did* bring it up first.

"So, we're going to do this?" I summarize.

"I'm in if you are."

"I'm in," I agree. "What exactly do we need to do?"

"More pictures together while we're on vacation to get the rumor mill working. Maybe after our beach getaway we could spend a little time in New York together and make sure we're seen? Nothing too inconvenient, just enough to get the rumor mill working."

"You really think anyone would care about you dating a washed up football player?"

"You might have a hard time believing this right now, but you are *so* much more than a washed up football player. You are a fucking gay icon, whether you like it or not. That's the only reason anyone gives a shit who your no-talent ex is sticking his dick in."

I chuckle and shake my head.

I can't believe we're doing this, but it *feels* like the right move, and if there's one thing I learned from football—it's to trust my gut instinct. It hasn't steered me wrong.

TRACK 16: SIDE A

Faking It

Benji

Waking up to the sound of birds singing and the salty smell of the ocean puts me in a good mood right away. The music of the island fills me up inside—the birds, the gentle crash of waves against the beach, chirping insects: it's a symphony of nature that calms everything inside me.

I roll over and stretch out in the large bed. The only thing that could make this morning better would be Paris in bed with me. I know, his idea of fake dating doesn't include fucking around, but that doesn't mean I can't fantasize a little.

Actually, now that I'm thinking about it, if we're really going to sell this thing, we need to commit.

I grab my phone off the nightstand along with my glasses, and slip out of bed in nothing but a pair of designer boxer briefs. I pad down the hall to the room Paris chose and tap on the door. When he doesn't answer, I turn the handle and slowly open it. He's sound asleep, sprawled out in the king-sized bed, navy blue sheets tangled around his legs, clinging to his ass in a way that should be illegal to looks so good.

He doesn't stir, so I tiptoe over to the bed and tap his bare shoulder, trying hard not to wonder if he's wearing anything under the sheet.

"Mmph?" he grumbles.

"I'm going to climb into bed and take a selfie with you in the background," I whisper, and he harrumphs again. Taking that as an okay, I carefully slide into bed next to him, positioning myself so you it looks like I just woke up and then holding the camera so I'm the focus but *oops, accidentally included the man in my bed in the background.* Then I take off my glasses and snap a few pictures. Putting my glasses back in place, I inspect the pictures for a few seconds after I take them. If anyone didn't see the picture yesterday of the two of us together, you wouldn't automatically know it's Paris in the background, and it's certainly going to start a frenzy of attention.

The description I add is entirely innocent, all about the things I might do today on vacation like hiking and swimming in the ocean, no mention of Paris. I'll let the picture speak for itself this time.

"Why are you in bed with me?" he asks in a groggy voice, thick with sleep and entirely too sexy.

"I was taking a picture."

"Of me?" He sounds borderline panicked.

"Only kind of. You were in the background as sort of a tease. It wasn't porny or anything."

"Still, we're going to have to explain to London why you're posting pictures of the two of us in bed naked together."

"I'm not naked," I point out. "Wait, are *you* naked?" My eyes flicker downward again to the sheet and the *very* clear outline of his dick.

"Why are you staring at my dick?" he asks, quickly moving a hand in front of it to obscure my view. *What a shame.*

"Um, because I love cock, and yours was practically on display through that thin sheet," I reason. "But what's the big deal about London? We'll tell him that we took his suggestion for the fake relationship thing, no big deal."

"I still don't get that," he says.

"Get what? It was your idea last night."

"No, I mean why London suggested I pretend to date you. It's weird coming from him, isn't it?"

"Why?"

"Because you guys used to date," he reasons.

"For the love of god," I groan. "Donnie and I never dated. Why can't anyone get that through their thick fucking skulls?"

"I literally walked in on him with his hands in your pants once," Paris reminds me.

"So?"

"What do you mean 'so'?"

"We used to jerk each other off sometimes, so what?" I shrug.

"That was it?"

"A couple of blowjobs too." I shrug.

"But you weren't dating?" Paris clarifies.
"You weren't in love and stuff?"

"I love your brother, but not like *that.*"

"This is serious? You *never* dated London?"

"Never," I repeat. "Why is this such a big
deal?"

I can see the wheels behind Paris' eyes
turning, but I can't figure out why he cares so
much that I never dated his brother.

"It's not a big deal; I'm just surprised." I can
tell he's not being completely honest, but I decide not to push it.

"What do you want for breakfast? I'll
cook."

"I usually don't eat a lot in the morning,
maybe just eggs, toast, and fruit?"

"You got it."

"I was thinking for going for a swim in the
ocean this morning. Swimming is great strength
building for my shoulder."

"Oh yeah, go, enjoy, I'll be on the back deck
having some coffee, and when you get back, I'll
make breakfast."

"Sounds good," he says, sitting all the way
up. I notice a wince as he puts pressure on his
shoulder, and I wonder just how bad it really is.

All the official reports say it's still uncertain if he'll be returning or not. But I know all too well about official reports and the shit we all tell reporters to get them off our backs.

It takes me a second to realize he's sitting there just staring at me like he's waiting for something.

"Oh shit, the naked thing, right." I jump up, giving him an apologetic smile before doing so.

"Hey, Benji," Paris calls before I reach the door to the bedroom.

"Yeah?"

"You look really cute in your glasses."

I roll my eyes at him. "I look like a nerd. I'm going to put my contacts in right now."

"I like them," he insists once more before I slip out of the room with a smile ghosting my lips.

Paris

The ocean swells and flows around me as I swim against the current. My shoulder throbs, but it's something I've gotten so used to over the past ten months I don't pay it much attention. I thought it would feel better by now, thought I'd be back to throwing the ball around at the very least, but every time I've tried, I can't get any power behind it. My PT told me to keep building up the strength in my rotator cuff to stabilize it, but it doesn't seem to be doing much good.

I let the water carry me back toward the

shore, and I start all over again, enjoying the workout and the chance to clear my head. Swimming laps in the ocean is a thousand times better than lifting weights in a gym that stinks of socks and sweat.

My mind is buzzing with a hell of a lot more than my predicament with my career though.

After Benji stepped out of my room, I pulled up his Instagram to see the picture he posted. The smile on his lips and the sleepy look in his hooded eyes was almost surreal; it looked so authentic. It was like having a window into an alternate dimension where Benji is actually my boyfriend, waking up in bed beside me in the morning.

And then there is the whole thing about him and London never dating. Maybe it doesn't matter at all, but I feel like everything has been turned upside down. It's like if someone told me two plus two is five. It fucks with you to have your truths rocked in such a way, and I've had more of that in the past year than most people can handle in a lifetime.

Pushing all the confusing thoughts from my mind, I focus instead on swimming. I let the waves of the ocean carry away the uncertainty and shattered realities and wash them out to sea. I swim until my muscles feel well used, and everything inside me begins to feel settled. When I drag myself out of the ocean, I feel more relaxed and centered than I've been since my injury. Apparently the ocean is a better therapist than the one the team sent me to see.

I use my hands to wipe the water from my face as I trudge through the sand toward the house, making a mental note to do some sand sprints this week too. As I near the house, Benji comes into view, sitting on the back deck as promised with a cup of coffee in one hand and a book in the other. His hair isn't pulled back anymore. Instead, it's hanging in long tendrils over his bare shoulders. He's not wearing anything but a pair of swim shorts, and my cock shifts in the confines of my own swim trunks as I take him in.

He glances up and smiles when he sees me. I'm a little disappointed to see he's not wearing his glasses anymore. They reminded me of cute, shy, teenage Benji. Not that confident, famous Benji isn't great too.

"Good swim?"

"Excellent," I say. "I'm going to hop in the shower quick, and then I'll join you out here."

"Great. I'll start breakfast."

After my shower, I put on a new pair of shorts and return to the porch where, as promised, Benji has fruit and eggs waiting, as well as a second steaming cup of coffee. I'm not sure why, but the gesture has emotion welling in my throat. I dated Elliot for years and never once did he ever make me breakfast and coffee. If this is what Benji does for someone he's pretending to date, I can only imagine how he treats genuine boyfriends.

"Wow, you take being a fake boyfriend really seriously," I joke to cover my sudden bout of wistfulness.

He chuckles and takes a sip of his own coffee, swiping a strawberry off my plate and popping it into his mouth.

"I'm not sure what you're in the mood to do today, but I thought I'd go for a hike. There's this waterfall that's supposed to be beautiful. I wanted to see it."

"I'm up for a hike," I agree, sliding into the seat beside Benji and picking at my plate of breakfast.

TRACK 17: SIDE A

Waterfalls

Benji

Sweat runs down my neck and has my shirt clinging to my back less than ten minutes into the start of our hike. Trees surround us as we make our way through the overgrown path, birds chattering overhead and creatures scurrying in the distant brush.

"Not to be *that* guy, but are you sure we're headed in the right direction? I don't particularly want to get lost in the rainforest."

"Where's your sense of adventure?" I tease.

"I lost it after watching one too many episodes of *I Shouldn't Be Alive*," Paris grumbles, and I laugh.

"I promise not to get us lost. And from what I hear, the view will be totally worth it once we get there."

"Trust me, I'm not complaining about the exercise. I just don't want my body to be discovered in six months picked over by scavengers."

"Dramatic," I accuse, throwing a smirk

over my shoulder.

Paris looks entirely too good covered in sweat, his shirt already removed and flung over his shoulder, his muscles taut and glistening. I lick my lips, and he arches an eyebrow at me.

"We should take another picture," I say quickly to cover up my shameless drooling over him. Reaching into my pocket, I pull out my phone and stand next to Paris. When I hold up the phone, he looks into the screen with me and frowns.

"Can you switch sides so you're covering my surgery scar?" he asks, and I shuffle around to his other side and snap a picture.

I take a look at it and frown. We look fine, but it feels like it's not quite enough. It's all well and good to say we're on vacation together, and of course there was the bed tease this morning, but I think we need to kick it up a notch to really get attention.

"One more," I say, holding the camera up again. Paris gets into position again, and this time, before I hit the button to snap the picture, I turn my head and press a kiss to his cheek.

The photo I captured is absolutely perfect. Paris is blushing, looking both surprised and pleased by the kiss.

"Damn, we look cute together," I declare before posting the picture to my Insta and Twitter and tagging him on both with a little caption about getting in touch with nature.

I put my phone back into my pocket, and we start walking again.

It takes another half hour for us to reach the waterfall; both of us are drenched in sweat and breathing heavily by the time we make it. We emerge from the trees at the base of the falls, the sound of rushing water loud as the sun reflects off the surface of the small lake.

I kick my shoes off and sit down on the edge of the water, sticking my feet in and moaning happily as the cool water surrounds them. Paris joins me within seconds, reaching into the water with both hands and splashing his face with it before sticking his feet in as well.

"I bet it would be fun to jump off from there into the little lake," Paris says, pointing at the ridge near the top of the waterfall.

"It would be dangerous," I argue. "Not that I'm opposed to dangerous, per se, but I'm pretty sure your sports agent would have an aneurysm if they knew you were doing something like that."

"Yeah," he agrees with a sigh.

"You think your ex's head is exploding yet from our pictures?" I ask to change the subject.

Paris chuckles. "Oh, I'm sure he's having an aneurysm. Not because he's jealous or wants me back, but because we're stealing his spotlight," he says. "What about you? Any exs who may be feeling jealous seeing you with someone new?"

"Hell no," I laugh. "I've never been very

good at dating," I confess.

"Oh?"

"Honestly, emotional connections give me hives."

Paris arches an eyebrow at me. "No offense, but that's bullshit."

"How so?"

"You have no problem forming emotional connections; look at you and London."

"That's not romantic," I argue.

"What's the difference?"

"I don't know," I lie.

"So, no boyfriends?" he asks again.

"Nope, none. Plenty of hookups, but no one serious," I say. "What do I need with serious anyway? I'm plenty happy on my own." I wonder if that sounds like less of a lie to Paris' ears than it does to mine.

We sit for a while, occasionally splashing ourselves or each other with water, talking about random topics and avoiding anything too serious, until we eventually decide it's time to head back.

Paris

"God, this is incredible," I murmur happily, stretching out on the chaise like a lazy cat. "I don't think I realized how much I needed this."

After we got back from our hike, we grabbed the bottle of tequila we started in on last night and a couple of limes, and then we headed back out onto the porch.

As far as I can tell, we're the only house for miles and miles. The silence of the late evening is broken only by the slapping of the ocean waves against the beach and the symphony of insects from nearby trees. Stars are just starting to twinkle above us as the pink and orange sunset fades from the horizon. I can't think of a single place in the world I'd rather be right now.

"Did you love him a lot?" Benji asks, and for a second I have no idea what he's talking about. A world exists outside of Benji and me here on this quiet beach?

"I thought I did, but when he left, I felt more relieved than anything, and I realized I couldn't have loved him much if it was such a weight off to have him gone," I confess. "I'm sure that makes me sound like a horrible person, but I'd spent *so* much time trying to be different for him, to make him happy, make him notice me and want me the way he used to. I didn't realize how exhausting that all was until he was gone."

"You don't sound horrible; that makes sense."

"And finding out he was cheating on me? It's more embarrassing than anything. I mean, there I was killing myself to make things work between us, and he was fucking someone else for *months*." Shame washes over me, and I wonder for a second if I should just walk straight into the ocean and let myself float away to escape the embarrassment of the confession.

Something brushes my shoulder, and I open my eyes to see Benji's long, slim fingers barely touching my skin. I lean into it.

"He's the one who should be ashamed, 'Ris."

"Yeah," I agree noncommittally, shrugging and feeling the weight of his hand as it follows the movement.

"No, listen to me," Benji says, his other hand finding my chin and turning my face so I'm looking right at him, the intensity of his forest green eyes boring into me. "You are incredible, and anyone would be lucky to be with you. I mean, god, that ass alone should make any man or woman fall at their knees to worship you."

His attention heats me all over. I can't tell if he means it or he's just trying to cheer me up, but it feels nice to hear all the same. I reach for the tequila and take a swig from the bottle then shake my head.

"I'm almost thirty with no idea of what to do with the rest of my life. I'm living in a shitty apartment in the middle of nowhere Ohio because I just don't know what else to do. It's not like I can't afford better, my bank account is pretty padded, but I'm afraid I'm going to have to live on what I have for the rest of my life. Football was *everything* to me; what do I do if I can't go back?"

"You pick yourself up and figure out where

you fit now. I know it's not easy. I know it fucking sucks, but you can't waste away forever feeling sorry for yourself."

"What if I don't fit anywhere?"

"Your life fell apart. Trust me, I can relate to how fucking scary that is, but instead of figuring shit out, you put on London's life, and now you're surprised it doesn't fit," Benji says. "Your brother *loves* that shitty little town with one stoplight and not much else, but it's not where you really want to be."

It's staggering how easily Benji sees right through me, and I'm not sure what to say. He reaches for the bottle of tequila in my hand, taking a gulp of his own. I watch with interest at the way his throat bobs when he swallows. The urge to lean forward and suck his Adam's apple is almost too much.

He hands it back, and I take another drink, the liquor warm as it hits my tongue and slides down my throat. It's not the same kind of burn that cheap tequila has; this is more pleasant.

"You think I should just pack up my apartment and move out when we get back to Ohio?"

"If you want to," he answers as if it's the easiest thing in the world.

"Where would I even go? People don't just move out of state without a plan, or a job, or a new place to live."

"Sure they do," he argues, taking the bottle from me again and taking another sip. "'Ris, the only person standing in your way right now is you. This is the one life you have; don't you owe it to yourself to make it fucking incredible?"

"Yes," I agree, my voice sounding husky to my own ears as my pulse thunders.

"So, what do you want more than anything?" he asks, rolling onto his side to face me.

Not a single thought passes through my mind before I do it. I'm all instinct and want, the gulps of tequila silencing the voice in the back of my mind that should surely be telling me it's wrong.

Benji gasps when my mouth meets his. His lips are soft and yielding under mine, parted easily by the sweep of my tongue. His hands find my pecs while I grab onto his hips, just above the low-slung waist of his swimsuit.

Our numb lips and tequila-soaked tongues slide against each other artlessly. A bead of sweat trickles down my back, the heat of the island suffocating enough without the raging inferno between the two of us. It's a wonder we don't burst into flames.

Benji moans into my mouth, climbing onto my lap without breaking the kiss, his slight body covering mine as our tongues tangle. My heart is going wild as my fingers dig into Benji's hips, feeling his cock as it hardens against my stomach.

I've replayed our one and only kiss over and over again throughout the years, the kiss that was never for me, and I was so sure I'd built it up to be better than it was. God was I wrong. Kissing Benji is like skydiving, exciting and terrifying all at once. It's like the first day of summer vacation, full of possibility and promise. It's *so* much better than I remembered.

Benji wraps his arms around my neck, kissing me back with equal enthusiasm. I tangle my fingers in his soft hair, thoroughly ruining his messy bun, and taste the depths of his mouth. I revel in the fact that I'm *allowed* to kiss him, that this time, he *knows* it's me.

TRACK 18: SIDE B

The Wrong Brother

Paris

The warm night caressed my skin as I leaned against the railing of my parents' porch, watching everyone throwing back drinks and celebrating freedom from high school. My eyes roamed around without my permission, seeking the strange, flamboyant boy who had occupied my every waking and sleeping thought for months. My brother's boyfriend.

I spotted him with a red Solo cup in his hand, wobbling across the lawn in my direction. I straightened up and clutched at the railing to keep myself from going to him and doing something truly stupid like confessing my feelings to him.

He looked up and a drunken, lopsided smile spread over his lips when our eyes met. I look around for London, expecting him to come by and intercept his boyfriend at any second before he could reach me, but he didn't come.

Benji reached me, throwing back whatever was in his cup and then tossing it carelessly in the direction of the garbage can a few feet from me.

"Can you believe we graduated?" he asked with a slur.

"No," I agreed, smiling and then reaching out to steady Benji as he swayed on his feet.

He looked down at my hand as it wraps around his elbow and let out a little giggle.

"I'll miss you."

Hope fluttered in the pit of my stomach. "I'll miss you too. I can't wait to hear your songs on the radio. Try not to forget me once you're rich and famous."

"I could never forget you," he said, a serious expression stealing over his face. "Did you know I loved you?"

My stomach plummeted as I realized he thought I was London.

"I...I..."

Before I could tell him I wasn't London, his lips were on mine, warm and demanding as they molded to my mouth. His hands gripped the front of my shirt, his body pressing flush against me, lighting me up like nothing I'd ever felt before. Nothing I've felt to this day, if I'm being honest.

I parted my lips, and his tongue slipped past them, teasing against mine and dragging a moan from my chest.

"Benji," I gasped when he pulled away.

"I need another drink," he declared, stumbling away like he didn't just rock my world on its foundation and tilt my life on its axis. I touched my fingers to my still tingling lips, watching him go, knowing that it might be the last time I'd ever see him. If all went well, I'd be in the NFL, he'd be touring the world, and our teenage years spent playing video games in a musty basement in Ohio would be nothing but a distant memory. I wouldn't forget the kiss though, that much I was sure of.

TRACK 19: SIDE A

Skinny Dipping

Benji

Paris kisses me until I'm breathless and so hard in my shorts I have no doubt the slightest breeze could make me come. I greedily run my hands all over his broad, firm chest and arms, being gentle when my fingers ghost over the rough scar on his right shoulder.

I'm not sure right now if I'm Paris' way of getting over what his ex did or if it's the tequila and vacation inhibitions. Whatever the hell inspired Paris to kiss me, I'm more than happy to go along for this ride.

He's as hard as I am, his erection pressing against my ass, his hands moving from my waist to my back and everywhere else he can seem to reach.

"Do you want to go for a swim?" I ask, pulling my lips from his and grinning down at him impishly. His mouth is wet and puffy from our kisses, and I have no doubt my chin is sporting some red whisker burn from his stubble.

He blinks in confusion for a few seconds,

trying to make sense of my suggestion. I climb off his lap and tug my shirt over my head, enjoying the way his gaze roams over my body appreciatively. Then I drop my shorts, and his eyes go wide.

"Last one in is a rotten egg," I say, shooting him a wink before turning and taking off down the beach at a dead sprint toward the ocean. It takes a few seconds before Paris is on my heels, cursing and stumbling to get his clothes off as we run.

I splash noisily into the water at full speed, stumbling as a wave crashes into me, knocking me back. I let the water flow over me before popping my head back to the surface and whipping around to see Paris diving into the ocean a few seconds behind me.

When he pops back up a few inches in front of me, I shoot him a smirk.

"I think you'd better officially retire from the NFL because that was embarrassing."

He splashes me, and I let out a peal of laughter, giving as good as I get.

"You cheated," he accuses.

"Sore loser," I shoot back with another burst of water in his direction.

Paris disappears under the waves again, and before I know it, his arms are around my waist, picking me up and launching me into the air before I come crashing back down into the water.

"Fuck," I hear him grunt as I resurface.

"You okay?" I swim closer to see him rubbing his shoulder.

"Yeah, I just shouldn't have done that. It's easy to forget sometimes how fucked my shoulder is."

"Is it okay; do you need anything?"

"I'll be all right," he assures me.

Another large wave crashes around us, pushing us toward the shore. We're dripping wet as we find our feet and stumble our way back onto the beach. Maybe drunk swimming wasn't the best idea, in all honesty.

I flop onto the sand and laugh, looking up at the night sky spread out above us infinitely. Paris plops down beside me, looking up at the sky as well. We turn our heads to look at each other at the same time, and we're kissing again—salty lips, hot tongues, lust coursing through our veins.

My achingly hard erection brushes his hip, and we both moan. Paris' hands tangle in my hair, tugging it like he can't decide if he's trying to stop me from kissing him or kiss me deeper.

"Benji," he murmurs against my lips.

"Hmm?" I pull back from his mouth and kiss my way down his throat, over his collar bone, nipping and licking at his damp skin.

"We should stop."

"Damn," I sigh, rolling onto my back to give him space.

"Sorry, my head is just fuzzy from the tequila, and everything feels so confusing right now; I need a minute to think."

I reach over and grab his hand, giving it a reassuring squeeze.

"You don't have to apologize. Both our lives are so up in the air right now. We're both trying to figure our shit out, and I'm sure the last thing either of us needs is anything complicated."

"So, if anything does happen between us, we can keep it casual?" Paris asks.

As much as I don't think I could do casual with the man I've had a crush on since the minute I first laid eyes on him, I was completely serious about neither of us needing anything complicated right now. We're both trying to figure out where our careers and futures are going and adding another person to that seems like the worst idea ever. "Yeah, I think casual would be the best idea."

"Let me think about it."

I turn back toward him and press a kiss to his cheek. "Take all the time you need," I say. "And in the meantime, I'm going to go in and take a shower because this sand is starting to itch."

He chuckles and gets to his feet. I look up at his naked body, looking incredible in the moonlight, glistening wet, his cock still hard. He holds a hand out to help me up, and I'm loathe to let it go once I'm on my feet, but I do.

We don't say anything else as we make our way back up to the house, parting ways when we reach our rooms.

One glance into the mirror tells me I'm a complete mess, covered in sand from head to toe, my hair tangled, the tie holding it in a bun now completely missing, my lips kiss swollen. My cock is still half-hard too, swaying between my legs. Turning away from my reflection, I reach into the shower to turn to water on, stepping under the spray without waiting for it to warm up.

As I soap my body to wash away the salt from the ocean and the sand from the beach, I imagine what it would have been like if Paris had decided to come to my room with me. It's too easy to fantasize about his body pressing against mine as the water from the shower beats down on us, rutting against each other as we continue the kissing from the beach.

I kissed him once before, but that was another lifetime ago. I doubt he even remembers it, but I certainly do. I've thought about that kiss a million times. I was drunk then too. I wonder what it's like to kiss Paris completely sober and if I'll ever get the chance to find out.

Once I'm free of sand, I step out of the shower and grab a towel off the shelf, hastily drying off before shuffling back into the bedroom and flinging myself into the huge bed and pulling the soft sheet over me. As soon as I close my eyes, images of Paris' gorgeous body continue to assault me, the taste of his mouth, the sound of his muffled moans against my lips.

I slip my hand under the thin sheet covering my waist and wrap it around my aching shaft. A moan falls from my lips, and I reach for my pillow to stifle the sound. The last thing I need is for Paris to hear me getting off, although it would be unbelievably fucking hot if he did. I tug at my cock, jerking myself slowly, rolling my hips and fucking into my fist to thoughts of Paris overhearing, growing hard at the sound of my moans, touching himself as he listens.

I groan into the pillow, biting down on the expensive pillowcase as I cant my hips and imagine Paris crawling onto the bed, positioning himself between my legs, and taking my cock into his throat.

"Fuck," I groan as my balls tighten, the pace of my hand increasing.

Paris

The squeak of the springs is the first thing that catches my attention. You'd think the walls would be practically soundproof in a house this expensive, but I can hear Benji's panting and moaning through the wall as if he was in bed right next to me.

My cock throbs, precum leaking from the slit and rolling down my shaft in heavy drips. My breath catches in my throat, and the pit of my stomach tightens with want. Putting the brakes on things down at the beach was hard enough, but hearing him get off is the ultimate test of my willpower. I swear I could drown in wanting him.

"*Fuck,*" I hear him groan, and I can't take it another second. Flinging the sheets off, I vault out of bed and practically sprint out of my bedroom, not bothering to stop and knock when I reach his door.

I push it open and nearly fall to my knees at the sight of Benji with a pillow half over his face to stifle his moans, his hand moving wildly beneath the thin sheet as he writhes in the bed. He doesn't even hear me come in, his eyes closed tightly as he chases his pleasure. My cock jerks, more precum beading at the tip.

I cross the room in a few quick strides and climb onto the foot of the bed. Benji gasps, finally realizing he's not alone, his grip on the pillow tightening as his eyes go wide. He pulls it away from his mouth, his hand stilling under the covers, his chest heaving with his heavy breaths.

"Paris, what are you—"

"Let me suck you off?"

He groans, throwing the covers back in invitation, and I waste no time wrapping my lips around him and taking his cock into my mouth. His shaft is hot against my tongue, the salty taste of his own precum bursting on my taste buds as

I lick him while hollowing my cheeks and suck-ing.

"Oh god, oh fuck," he moans, running his fingers through my short hair and tugging at it. His thighs fall open wide, and his back arches as the crown of his cock breaches my throat, and I swallow around him.

I run my hands along his thighs, feeling his coarse hair under my palms, his muscles tens-ing and trembling as I work my mouth up and down his erection, throating him over and over. I hump against the bed, seeking relief of my own as his cock thickens against my tongue, growing even harder as my name falls from his lips over and over again like a chant.

The first spurt of his release hits the back of my throat, and I swallow eagerly, sucking harder as his orgasm pulses against my tongue, my own balls tightening as I fuck my cock against the silky sheets until my own orgasm rips from me.

I release Benji from my mouth and rest my head against the inside of his thigh as I ride out the aftershocks of my own orgasm, his fingers still stroking through my hair.

"Sorry, I came all over your sheets," I apologize with a tired laugh once I'm able to talk again.

"I'm not complaining."

I turn my head and press a kiss to his leg, noticing a tattoo with French words scrawled there.

"What's it say?" I ask, running the pad of my index finger over the curvy letters.

"*Je Suis*, it means, *I am* in French."

"What's it mean?"

He snorts a laugh. "It means that when I'm drunk, I buy into my own hype a little too much sometimes."

I crawl out from between his legs, shuffling up the bed until I'm next to him. He rolls toward me, resting his head on my shoulder, his hair wet from the shower he took when we got in, his skin still flush from his pleasure.

"I don't understand."

"I got it after a night of drinking in Paris. I don't know what I wanted it to mean at the time, but once I sobered up it felt really pretentious."

"Well, I kind of like it," I say with a shrug.

"Thank you," he whispers. "And thank you for the blowjob."

"I'm still not sure if this is a good idea," I admit. "I heard you through the wall, and I made an impulsive decision, but…"

"'Ris, we said casual, so let's not make this a big thing. We're on vacation, anything we do here doesn't count anyway, right?"

I chuckle. "What happens on the island stays on the island?"

"Exactly."

"Okay," I say after a few seconds of considering it. My physical therapist *did* tell me to relax and have some fun; this is practically doctor's orders.

As soon as I kissed him earlier, I knew I was going to have to see where things might go. And if Benji is willing to keep things casual while we both work on holding our crumbling lives together, I can't see a reason to say no. "I should go to my bed."

"You don't have to," he says. "I mean, if you want to stay, it's cool."

"Okay," I say again, settling in with his head resting on my good shoulder and closing my eyes.

TRACK 20: SIDE A

Going Down

Benji

The sound of my phone vibrating on the nightstand beside me pulls me out of a deep sleep, and I grumble. With Paris' larger body wrapped around me, the last thing I'm worried about is whoever's calling. The buzzing stops, and I smile, snuggling back closer to Paris, feeling his morning wood pressing against the curve of my ass. He groans as I wiggle into him, tightening his arms around me and pressing his lips to the back of my shoulder.

My phone starts to go off again, and I curse under my breath.

"Ignore it," Paris mumbles sleepily.

"They've already called at least twice," I whisper, grabbing for my phone while maintaining as much contact with Paris as I can manage. "It's your brother."

He stiffens behind me and not in the good way.

"It's London?"

"Yeah, relax. He's probably just calling to

gloat that we went with his suggestion after all," I assure him, hitting the button to accept the call. "Do you have any idea what time it is?" I complain to London as soon as I answer.

"I'm pretty sure it's noon where you are," he answers.

"Oh, I guess that's a reasonable time to call then."

"Are you still asleep?" he asks.

"I'm on vacation."

"You're whole life is a vacation," he jokes.

"I wish," I grumble. "If you think being crammed onto a tour bus with four other men, living with the smell of dirty socks and enough emotional baggage to fill a whole second tour bus is a vacation, you need your head examined."

"Fair enough," London chuckles. "So, who's better in bed, me or Paris?"

"You know, I'm starting to think you've got some sort of twincest fantasy with how obsessed you are with your brother's sex life."

Paris starts to cough, and I try to cover the phone so London won't hear him.

"Dude, is he in bed with you right now?"

"No, the walls are super thin," I lie. "We're not hooking up. We're faking it for publicity like you suggested."

"Really? That's it?"

"Sorry to disappoint. Now if that's all you called about, I've gotta go take a piss and make some coffee."

"Yeah, I'll talk to you later."

I hang up and toss my phone down on the bed as I slip out and head for the bathroom.

After I relieve my bladder and brush my hair and teeth, I head back into the bedroom, thinking about ways we could start the morning right. Number one on the list is returning the favor from last night and sucking Paris off. But, when I get there, I find the bed empty, the rumpled sheets the only evidence he was ever there.

I pull on a pair of shorts and go in search of him. The smell of coffee lures me to the kitchen where I find Paris with a frown on his face as he uses the grinder on coffee beans. My stomach twists, and my heart plummets. So much for spending the next five days in a haze of incredible sex.

"You're regretting last night?" I guess, figuring if I say it first it'll hurt less.

"You said he wouldn't care."

"What?"

"You said you and London never dated, and he wouldn't care if we messed around," Paris clarifies.

"He won't. Did you not hear that he was calling to ask if we'd had sex?"

"Then why'd you lie?" he asks. "If it's not a big deal, why didn't you want him to know I was in your bed?"

"Shit, 'Ris, it's not because I thought Donnie would flip out or anything. Honestly, I thought he'd be too excited about it. You and I can agree that this is casual all we want, but if he knows we're hooking up, he's going to be emotionally invested in it."

The muscle in Paris' jaw twitches, and his shoulders seem to relax a little.

"That's all? You're not ashamed? We're not doing anything behind his back to hurt him?"

My heart warms at his concern for his brother. I round the counter and, when he turns to face me, I wrap my arms around his waist, pressing myself against him so I have to tilt my head a little to look right at him.

"I love Donnie; I wouldn't do anything to hurt him," I promise. Another little frown tugs at his lips and, since I'm here, I take the liberty of kissing this one away. "You got out of bed too fast; you should go back," I tempt, pressing myself against him suggestively.

"Oh yeah, what will we do in bed?" he flirts, wrapping his arms around me and grabbing my ass with both hands as he nips at my bottom lip.

"Mmmm, I think we can come up with something."

Wiggling out of his grasp, I grab his hand and tug him out of the kitchen, back to my bedroom, excitement blooming in the pit of my stomach. Last night we were drunk on tequila and lust; it could easily be written off. Fooling around in the sober light of day has an entirely different meaning to it.

Paris crawls into my bed, shucking his shorts and tossing them onto the floor while I step out of mine and climb on top of him. Our lips meet again in a frenzy of hard kisses and groping hands, our naked bodies sliding against each other, hard everywhere we're pressed together.

"So fucking sexy," I murmur against his lips as I dig my fingers into his muscles and grind my erection against his. I kiss my way down his jaw, his throat, until I reach the large, angry scar on his right shoulder and place a gentle kiss there as well. It was obvious on Christmas that he's still struggling with what happened, and there are a million questions I'm dying to ask about it, but now is obviously not the time.

I continue to explore his body with my mouth—biting his nipples, sucking on the ribbed edges of his abs, dipping my tongue into his belly button. The head of his cock bumps against my chin as I suck a bruise just below his belly button. Paris' hands tangle in my hair, tugging it as he gasps and laughs at each lick and nibble of his stomach. His hips twitch, and his cock bumps my chin again.

"Are you trying to tell me something?" I tease, dragging my tongue along the muscled ridges of his hips.

He chuckles again and then moans when I

bite down gently. "I mean I wouldn't be *mad* or anything if you decided to suck my dick."

I push his thighs farther apart and kiss my way between them, my mouth on his hairy legs, learning the contour of each muscle and finding all of his ticklish spots. Wrapping my hand around his thick shaft, he groans and bucks into my touch. I pump him slowly, more of a tease than anything, as I suck another bruise on the inside of his left thigh, and he starts to tremble slightly. My hand grows slick with his precum as it leaks from his slit and drips down his length until it meets my pumping fist.

"Benji," he moans, and I smile against his skin.

When something starts to buzz, he stills and looks down at me with an arched eyebrow.

"What the fuck is that?" he asks.

"I was just going to ask you the same thing." It stops, and I'm about to brush it off and move on to making Paris fall apart in my mouth. But then the buzzing starts up again. "Oh, shit, that must be my phone."

I sit up and glance around the large, messy bed trying to see where I tossed it earlier.

"If that's London calling again, I'm going to kill him," he murmurs as I spot my phone and reach for it.

"Ugh, worse, it's Archer." I think about ignoring it but considering how adamant he was about us all taking a vacation, I'm worried the only reason he'd be calling is if something catastrophic happened. I hit the accept button and say hello.

"You didn't think you should let me or the PR firm know that you were suddenly going to start dating the most famous and talked about football player in America?"

"Damn, I knew I was forgetting something," I say lightly, mouthing *sorry* at Paris.

"I got a pissed off call from Sean. He says his phone has been ringing off the hook asking for details about the relationship from every gossip site in existence. Needless to say, he wasn't thrilled when I told him I didn't know a damn thing about it."

"Sorry, it all happened so fast," I answer honestly. It's not like we gave a ton of thought to this whole fake dating thing, and I've never dated anyone in the spotlight before to know that this was something to let my PR guy, Sean, know about.

"It's fine," Archer says, his voice softening. "I thought you were dating this guy's brother though."

I pinch the bridge of my nose and growl. "As soon as I hang up the phone with you, I'm taking out a fucking billboard that says *Benji never dated London* in the middle of Times Square."

Paris chuckles, drawing my attention back to him. His erection is starting to wane, but his legs are still spread around me, so I take the liberty of running my free hand up his thigh and cupping his balls. He lets out a quiet gasp, and I bite my lip against a laugh while Archer goes on about something on the other end of the phone.

"Are you even listening?" he asks eventually.

"Nope," I admit, moving from his balls to wrap my hand around his shaft again, loving the way he hardens under my touch, his head falling back against the pillow as he bites his lip against a moan.

"You're having sex while you're on the phone with me? Have you been learning from Jude?" he asks dryly, and I instantly feel bad.

"Sorry, Arch." I stop stroking Paris. "I'll email a statement to Sean within the hour that he can give to any gossip site that wants to know."

"Thank you," he says. "And, for what it's worth, you look really happy in your Instagram photos."

I glance down at Paris again and smile. "Thanks. Now I have a very naked man in my bed I'd love to attend to, so I'll talk to you later."

"Later."

I hang up my phone and toss it in the direction of my shorts, in a heap on the floor, and then lean forward to wrap my lips around Paris' cock. He burrows his fingers into my hair and moans loudly as I take him as deep as I can, using my hand around the base to jerk him as I suck and bob my head up and down his shaft. I've dreamed about Paris' cock in my mouth since I was fifteen, and it's even better than I imagined.

It doesn't take long before he's pulsing against my tongue, hot, sticky bursts of cum hitting the back of my throat. I swallow every drop and then lick the over-sensitive head of his cock to make sure I haven't missed a drop.

As soon as I pull off of him, he hauls me up and flips me over, sucking me off like he did last night—with enthusiasm and *plenty* of skill— until I'm shouting and coming down his throat as well.

"Are you in trouble with your manager?" he asks once we both have a chance to catch our breath and come down from the high of our orgasms.

"Nah, I just have to send an email to my PR guy."

"I guess I'd better do that too. Should we write it together, so our statement is the same?"

"Yeah, but first, coffee," I declare, climbing out of bed, not bothering with any clothes this time before heading out of the bedroom for the kitchen.

TRACK 21: SIDE A

Island Music

Paris

After coffee and breakfast, Benji and I sit down to write out a statement for our publicists. We keep it short and sweet, saying we've been friends since high school, and when we saw each other for Christmas this year, sparks flew. We add a few more vague sentences to add intrigue and declare it good. Then, we take another picture together to post on Instagram.

"What do you feel like doing today?" Benji asks once all of our *business* stuff is out of the way.

Honestly, the only thing I can think of doing is dragging him back to bed and making the most of whatever is going on between us. We vaguely agreed that this doesn't count as anything since we're on vacation, so that means everything ends when we step foot back in Ohio, right? It should; I know we both have too much else to worry about right now. But it feels like the two-minute warning has been called when the game is only just starting.

"Whatever you want."

"I'd love to go check out the little town not far from here," he says.

"Works for me," I agree. "Mind if I go for a quick swim and grab a shower first?"

"Go right ahead. I'll lay out and get some sun until you're ready."

An hour later, we're getting into the same car that dropped us off at the house two days ago —has it really only been two days?—and heading for town.

"Is your shoulder okay, by the way?" he asks.

"My shoulder?" I reach instinctively for my injured shoulder, the memory of tossing him in the water last night coming back to me. "Oh yeah, I probably shouldn't have done that, but it feels okay. Well, as okay as it ever feels anymore," I admit with a grimace.

"How long before it's fully healed?"

I turn toward the window to look out at the beautiful scenery flying past, because it's much easier than looking at Benji when he's asking questions like that.

"Not sure, I need to keep strengthening it. It's sort of a wait and see kind of a thing."

"Oh, I thought they were expecting you back next season."

"They are," I say with a sigh. "Honestly, the not knowing is the worst part. If I knew for sure my career was over, then I could plan for a different future, but right now, I have no idea what's going to happen. All I can do is keep working and hoping."

Benji's hand touches mine tentatively. I flip my hand over so it's palm up, and he slips his fingers between mine, giving a comforting squeeze. Even without any more words between us, it's the most settled I've felt since I felt my cartilage tear and my shoulder come out of the socket.

The town isn't what I expected. I had pictured a tourist trap filled with people on vacation crawling all over, overpriced restaurants, and t-shirt stands. There was none of that.

"The closest resort is on the other side of the island. Aside from beach houses owned by rich assholes"—Benji shoots me a wry smile —"it's just locals in the area."

"This is kind of nice," I admit as we walk down the sunny, quiet street, the back of our hands or our arms brushing every so often, keeping me keenly aware of his proximity.

We stop into several small shops, and Benji buys a number of trinkets and a few expensive collectables, arranging to have them all shipped back to his penthouse in New York. I've made decent money in the NFL, but I have no doubt that Benji is in a whole other universe when it comes to his bank account. He also buys himself a gourd that's been turned into some kind of instrument. This one he keeps rather than having shipped home.

"What's it like being a huge rock star?" I ask curiously as we start to walk again.

Benji chuckles and shrugs. "What's it like being a star quarterback?"

I roll my eyes. "I'm an *average* quarterback who no one would even be talking about if it weren't for the fact that I'm out."

"You know, I wanted to call you so badly when you did that coming out interview," he confesses.

"Why didn't you?"

He shrugs again, biting down on his lip and furrowing his eyebrows. "I figured you didn't want to talk to me. You'd been avoiding me since I left on our first tour, even when London and I went to see you play in that college bowl thingy, you were too busy to hang out afterward."

I scrunch my nose, feeling like a total asshole. I thought my reasons for steering clear of Benji after that drunken kiss on graduation night were solid, but it clearly hurt his feelings. "I'm sorry I was an asshole. I would've liked it if you'd called, and I'm sorry you felt like you couldn't."

"You were so fucking brave," he says. "Every time I saw a hateful comment on social media, I nearly went postal. Archer had to ban me from Tweeting for six whole months because he was afraid I'd stir up too much drama."

I chuckle and resist the urge to reach for his hand. I'm not sure how well that would be re-

K.M. NEUHOLD

ceived around here or by Benji for that matter.

"You never answered my question."

"What's it like to be a rock star?" he repeats with another laugh. "Honestly? It's fucking awesome. Stepping out onto that stage to screaming fans, hearing our songs on the radio, our faces on t-shirts...it's the greatest feeling in the world." There's a hint of sadness behind the words, and I glance over to see his eyes looking wistful and resigned.

He's living his dream and watching it slip away before his eyes. I can more than relate.

"I'm starving; let's get something to eat," he suggests, quickly changing the subject before beelining for a little restaurant up ahead.

Benji

After our day of exploring the little town, we end up back home on the porch again, eating, drinking, and laughing as lustful tension slowly builds between us again as the night wears on.

"How do you even play that thing?" Paris asks, eyeing the shekere—the gourd instrument —I bought in town.

"It's easy; I'll show you." I pick up the instrument, holding it by the neck with one hand and demonstrating how to do the pound then shake motion to create a tempo, using the music of the island—the ocean, the birds, the insects— to harmonize. He bobs his head to the beat, and after a few minutes, I hold it out for him to try.

There's no nice way to say it: the man lacks rhythm. He can't quite seem to get a proper beat going, more of a haphazard thumping and off tempo shake until he gets frustrated and hands it back over.

"You made that look so easy," he complains.

"And I'm sure if you were showing me how to throw a football, you'd make that look easy," I say.

"I guess," he agrees. "You just seem to find a beat so easily."

"You just have to listen to the music all around you and find the rhythm."

"I don't hear any music," he says with a laugh.

"Sure you do. Quiet for a second, just listen."

We both grow silent, and Paris gets the cutest look of concentration on his face as he tries to hear what I'm hearing. I take the instrument back and listen to the crash of the ocean waves again for a few seconds before I start to shake the gourd to the same beat.

"Hear that, the ocean?" I prompt, nodding to the shekere and then at the waves. "And then listen to the birds; they're giving us the melody." I change the rhythm I'm shaking to harmonize with the birds instead.

"It all just sounds like noise to me," he admits. "How'd you learn how to play so many instruments?"

"I'm obsessed with instruments from different cultures and musical styles. I collect a lot of different things, but instruments are my favorite. The shekere originated in South Africa; I already have a few at home," I explain. "When I can, I try to learn how to play from the people I buy the instruments from, but sometimes I have to rely on YouTube videos or just figuring it out myself."

"What other instruments do you have?"

"Oh tons, a sitar, didgeridoo, bassoon, a zurna, to name a few," I list off a few of my favorites.

"Wow."

"Music is my life," I say with a shrug. "Before I transferred to Jefferson and met you and London, I was bullied pretty badly. Music was my escape. I spent lunch period in the band room with the band teacher. When I'd get home at the end of the day, I'd go up to my room and either listen to music or play it. I loved being able to pour my emotions into it, get lost in it; it's cathartic."

"I get that." Sadness crosses his features, and without giving myself time to weigh the pros and cons, I climb over into his chair with him, tucking myself against his chest when he opens his arms for me.

"How do we find ourselves again when the thing the defines us disappears?" I ask the question that's been plaguing me for nearly a year out loud for the first time.

"I'm not sure," he admits. "I think we need to find new ways to define ourselves?"

"Easier said than done," I sigh.

"It absolutely is."

"Alternative suggestion, we get lost in orgasms and pretend our problems don't exist for another few days?"

Paris' chuckle rumbles against me, and he slips a hand into my shorts to cup my ass.

"I'm totally game for that."

TRACK 22: SIDE A

New Year, New You

Benji

The past two days have been filled with nothing but sun, sand, and blowjobs. Best. Vacation. Ever. I glance over at Paris, asleep in the bed beside me. He looks peaceful and sexy as hell, his body naked, the sheet tangled around his legs, leaving all the interesting bits free for me to ogle as I wait for him to wake up.

I still can't believe after all these years of pathetically crushing on him, he's actually naked in my bed. I've had his cock in my mouth. I've touched and cuddled and kissed him. If I didn't know any better, I'd think our plane crashed into the ocean on the way to the island, and this is heaven.

I have no idea what's going to happen when we get home, but at the very least, I think we'll be closer now. Maybe it won't be ten years before I see him again. This could be the start of a beautiful friendship. I try not to feel disappointed at the thought. I'd love to be friends with Paris, and we'll certainly need to be, at least for a little while if we're doing this fake boyfriend thing.

Fake dating has been working like a charm too. We're both trending on Twitter, we've each nearly doubled our Instagram followers, and the gossip sites can't stop speculating about us. We posted more pictures yesterday, including a couple where we're kissing. No one is talking about Paris' injury, and for once, people are paying attention to me rather than Lincoln or Jude, it's a win-win.

Paris groans and stretches, all of his muscles twitching.

"Morning," I say, and he groans again, reaching for me without opening his eyes and dragging me against him. Plastered against his muscles, slightly sweaty from the heat and from sleep, the scent of him wrapping around me, I'm certainly not complaining.

"Sex or breakfast first?" I ask, reaching between his legs and wrapping my hand around his swollen shaft. He moans, twitching his hips and pressing his face into the crook of my neck.

"Is that even a question?" Paris' teeth graze my throat. "God, what are you doing to me? I swear I wasn't this insatiable when I was eighteen."

He rolls over on top of me, and I release my hold on his cock as it presses against my own. I wrap my legs around his waist and hold on for the ride as he thrusts against me, hot, hard steel of his morning wood against mine.

"Back at you. It must be the island; there's an aphrodisiac in the water or something," I reason breathlessly, not wanting to admit the intensity of my crush on him or think about what it could mean that he's feeling the same way I am.

"Mmm, must be," he agrees before kissing me. Morning breath be damned, we share a deep, hungry kiss as Paris humps against me, precum from both of our cocks mixing to slick the way slightly as we moan into each other's mouths.

My cock throbs as he fucks against it, my fingers digging into his back as my toes curl, and my back arches. It feels so good. Too good. Too fucking good.

"Paris, oh god," I groan against his mouth as my balls draw tight, heat pooling in the pit of my stomach and spreading through my body, my breath coming in short bursts before a keening cry falls from my lips, and my cock starts to pulse against his, my orgasm coating both our stomachs.

Paris isn't far behind me, rutting faster against my pumping cock until he growls, and his release joins mine in making us sticky.

"Fuck, that was hot," he says before collapsing on top of me.

I chuckle and kiss the side of his face. "Come on, let's go shower, and then I'll make breakfast," I suggest, wiggling under him so he'll move and stop crushing me, as if his body weight pinning me down isn't the best thing I've felt in my life.

He grumbles but rolls off of me.

We enjoy a second round of orgasms in the shower before managing to get our hands off each other and actually get clean.

Once we're clean, dry, and semi-dressed, we head into the kitchen for breakfast.

"Do you want to do anything special for New Year's Eve tonight?" I ask as I cut up some fruit.

"Honestly, I can't think of anything better than how we've already been spending this vacation."

"So, booze and sex to ring in the new year?" I ask with a wolfish grin.

"Sounds perfect."

Paris

After breakfast, I go for a swim in the ocean like I've been doing all week, and then we decide to go for another short hike to explore the island a little.

Benji chatters away about the musical culture of the US Virgin Islands, and I find myself hanging on his every word, not because I'm particularly interested in the topic, but because his excitement about it is infectious. The way his face lights up as he talks about how music shapes things from religion to cultural traditions and just about everything else is captivating, and I know I'm getting way too emotionally invested in a man who I agreed to be casual with. I can't seem to put on the brakes though as my heart sets a course for disaster.

A red flower catches my eye, and I stop to admire it for a few seconds before picking it.

"That's a pretty flower," Benji says. "I think it's a hibiscus."

"Come here," I wave him closer, and he comes. I tuck a strand of his long, silky hair behind his ear and then nestle the flower there as well. The smile that spreads on his lips is soft and sweet, and I can't resist stealing a kiss to taste his happiness.

"Take a picture for Instagram?" he asks when I pull back, and just like that, the moment crumbles. None of this is real. We may be playing that it is in more way than one, but at the end of the day, it's all a show and a vacation fling, nothing more.

"Of course," I say with a forced smile, pulling out my phone to take a picture and posting it on my social media sites with a sappy caption.

He leaves the flower in his hair as we keep walking, and I push away the sick feeling of disappointment trying to take root in the pit of my stomach. We've been having a great time; there's no reason to ruin it with *what ifs*.

After our hike, we head back to the house and raid the kitchen to decide what to make for dinner. We settle on grilling some fish, gathering all the items we need and heading onto the back porch where we've spent a majority of our vacation when we haven't been in bed.

We spend the next few hours eating and talking as we wait for midnight to come. Benji tells me fabulous stories featuring impressive people, and I relive some of my glory talking about football. My heart aches a little to talk about it when the future is so uncertain, and Benji never pushes for more than I want to talk about. I can't believe how much of each other's lives we've missed in the past ten years, and at the same time, it feels like we haven't skipped a beat. Whatever else happens between us, I make a promise to myself not to lose any more time with him, even as friends.

"Happy New Year," Benji says when midnight hits, holding his glass up so I can clink mine against it.

"Happy New Year," I respond, leaning in and pressing a brief kiss to his lips.

We sit back in our chairs and look up at the starry night sky. The sound of fireworks thunder in the distance, but neither of us bother turning around to try to see them.

"Usually I think the whole *New Year, New You* stuff is bullshit, but I think a fresh slate is exactly what I need," I admit, lifting my glass to my lips to take a sip of the fruity cocktail Benji whipped up for both of us because he said it was more festive for New Year than tequila straight from the bottle.

"Oh yeah, what kind of new you are you thinking? Because I'm kind of partial to the one who's already here."

"I don't know if I'm going to be able to play football or not anymore, and it's time I started thinking about what else I can dedicate my life to."

Benji falls quiet, and I glance over to see him looking pensive and sad.

"It's probably immature, but I keep thinking that if I pretend the band isn't falling apart, then it can't really happen. I don't know what I'm going to do if we don't sign a new contract with Epic. Music is my entire life."

"I know the feeling," I sigh. "I've thought a lot about finding a way to still be a voice for LGBT athletes. Maybe a foundation or...I don't know, would it be crazy if I wanted to open my own PR firm or sports agency specifically for LGBT athletes?"

"I don't think that's crazy at all; I think it would be awesome."

"Yeah? I also thought about maybe going to high schools to give inspirational speeches or whatever, talk to the kids about diversity and anti-bullying type stuff. Talk about being an openly gay football player."

Benji's gets up off his chair and squeezes into mine with me, kissing my shoulder and then laying his head there.

"I think that's an amazing idea," he says. "I've been thinking a lot about starting some sort of LGBT organization for teens. I haven't had time to think about the details much, but if the band splits, at least I'll have plenty of time to focus on that."

"That sounds like a lot of work," I hedge. "Almost like it would be a two man job."

"Yeah?" I can hear the smile in his voice. "Know anyone who might want to help with it?"

"I'll ask around for you," I tease, kissing the top of his head, and then, because things are getting way too heavy, I slip a hand under his shorts to cup his ass. "I think you said something about ringing in the new year with orgasms?"

"One track mind," Benji grumbles, but his smile gives him away as he slithers down my body, frees my cock, and takes it into his mouth without any teasing.

Happy New Year indeed.

TRACK 23: SIDE A

All Good Things Come to an End

Benji

Waking up on the last morning of our vacation is bittersweet. Sure, I still have a naked Paris in bed with me, but tomorrow morning we go home and everything that's happened over the past week is going to feel like a fever dream.

"You know what I want to do today," Paris says as soon as he opens his eyes.

"What's that?"

"I want to go back to that waterfall and jump into the lake."

"I thought we agreed that was dangerous and would give your agent a heart attack?"

"I don't care. Chances are I'm not going to be able to play again anyway, and I could stand a little danger right about now. I want to take a risk. I want to jump and feel a rush of excitement before I hit the water."

I'm not sure if he's talking specifically about the waterfall or if there's a metaphorical meaning behind his words as well, but his eyes are lighting up at the thrill. I can't find it in myself to argue because everyone needs excitement in their life.

"Okay, let's do it."

We share a shower like we have every day for the last five days and then have breakfast before heading out for our hike to the waterfall. We walk in silence today, unlike yesterday, and I wonder if our looming trip home is on his mind as much as it's on mine. I almost open my mouth to bring it up several times, to ask what he wants to have happen once we're back in Ohio, but I chicken out each time.

We can hear the babble of the waterfall more than a mile out, and Paris speeds up. I don't want to dwell on things ending tomorrow, so instead I decide to make the most of our last day together. Sneaking up behind him, I give him a pinch on the ass and then dart around him when he protests, running ahead a few yards before calling back to him over my shoulder, "Last one there is a rotten egg."

"Cheater," he yells before he breaks out into a run to catch up with me.

I burst through the trees only a few steps ahead of him, both of us laughing. I stop and put my hands on my knees, trying to catch my breath but he seems perfectly fine.

"You need to build up your endurance," he says, and I give him the finger.

"Fuck, I'm out of shape."

"You'll live. Come on, let's see if there's a

good trail up there."

I huff out a few more breaths before straightening up and following him. There is a trail that leads up to the top of the falls. It's not too high, but certainly high enough to give me a little flutter of nerves in my chest when we reach the spot Paris wants to jump from.

"You sure about this 'Ris?" I ask as I look down at the water below.

"It'll be fine; don't worry," he assures me.

"Fine, but I'm going first." I take off my shoes, holding them in one hand as I step up to the edge.

Paris rolls his eyes but doesn't argue as I step up to the ledge. I glance down at the water again, my heart hammering fast and hard against my ribcage, and then I turn my head to smirk at Paris over my shoulder.

"If I die, tell London I loved him," I tease, and he scowls. I blow him a kiss and launch myself off the ledge.

For a few heart pounding seconds, I fall through the air, hoping like hell he was right and that the jump wasn't too high to be safe. When my body hits the semi-cool water beneath me, I hold my breath and let the water surround me. By the time I kick back to the surface, shoes miraculously still in hand, a laugh bursts from my lips, and I let out a loud *whoop*.

"That was fucking awesome!" I shout up to Paris who's watching from above.

"Told you you'd be fine."

"Yeah, yeah. Now jump!" I call.

"Give me a second; it's high as fuck."

"Oh, come on, you big baby; this was your idea."

"I'm doing it," he assures me.

"Do a cannonball," I suggest. "No, wait, do a backward fall; that would be fun."

Paris seems to consider my suggestions before turning around so his back is to me and slowly moving to the edge.

"Jump, jump, jump," I chant gleefully just as he takes one more step. But instead of springing off, his foot stumbles like he hadn't realized how close he was. My heart stops, and time seems to slow down around me as he fumbles to keep himself from falling. His arms flail, and he grabs onto a small outcropping.

"Mother fucker," he curses before releasing his grip and falling the rest of the way down. I hold my breath and thank god when he hits the water without bouncing off any of the rocks jutting out from the side.

I swim in the direction of where he landed as fast as I can, unable to breathe until I see him burst through the surface of the water again unscathed.

"Are you okay?"

"Fuck, no. I fucked up my shoulder," he groans. "Mother fucking shit fucker," he swears as he starts to swim toward land, and I follow him.

As soon as he climbs out of the water, I gasp. It's obvious his right shoulder is out of the socket, his arm hanging limply at an odd angle by his side.

"Shit, shit, shit." I scramble out of the water. "Okay, we're going to get you to the hospital in town. Are you going to be okay to get there?"

Paris lets out a pained laugh. "I'm used to playing through the pain; I'll be fine."

Paris

The next few hours go by in a blur of pain as we hike back to the house, and Benji calls us a ride to town, asking over and over again if I'm okay. I grunt responses at him, trying to compartmentalize the pain and not consider what this means for my career, even though I have a feeling I already know the answer to that.

Benji waits in the waiting area while I go with the doctor to have my shoulder put back in place and images taken. I explain to him about my previous injury, and he agrees to do a phone consult with the orthopedic surgeon who did my original surgery. I'm not sure how long I'm there, but it feels like an eternity, and all I can think about is how I'm wasting our last day here. I'm too numb to think about anything else.

"Oh my god, I'm sorry, I'm sorry, I'm sorry," Benji says as soon as I step out of the doctor's office, my arm in a sling. "This is all my fault."

I arch an eyebrow at him. "How do you figure it's your fault? I'm the one who suggested we jump, and I'm the dumbass who slipped."

"But I wanted to go back to the waterfall, and I was cheering you on to jump," he argues. "What did the doctor say? How bad is it?"

"Pretty bad," I admit. "He sent the x-rays to my orthopedic surgeon, and they got on a conference call about it. Apparently, my labrum re-tore."

"Oh shit."

"He said there's too much scar tissue for another surgery so it's going to be rest and more PT," I go on.

"What does this mean for your career?" Benji asks in a hushed voice like he's almost afraid to say it out loud.

"Oh, that's over," I say, feeling an eerie sort of calm creeping over me.

"Fuck."

"Pretty much," I agree with a humorless chuckle. "But, hey, at least I know now."

Benji studies me carefully, his eyes roaming over my face as a frown forms on his lips. "It's okay to be upset about this; you don't have to put on a brave face."

"I'm not upset."

He backs off after that, and I sink into myself, wrapping the numbness around me like a blanket. I'm sure it's part shock, part pain meds, but it's better than letting myself feel the weight of knowing my career in football is really and truly over now.

We're both silent on our ride back to the beach house.

"Do you want dinner?" Benji offers carefully as we step inside the house. I can tell he's waiting for me to explode into either anger or tears at any moment.

"Actually, the pain meds the doctor gave me are making me pretty tired. I think I'm going to go lay down in my room."

"Oh." Disappointment flickers over his face, but I can't deal with that right now, so I turn away and make my way down the hallway to the bedroom I only slept in on the first night here.

With a detached sort of interest, I notice my hand shaking as I pull the door closed behind me. I vaguely make a mental note that my clothes are still damp from the lake earlier, but I can't find any interest in bothering to take them off, instead crawling into bed and pressing my face into my pillow. As soon as I do, a sob racks my body, the numbness falling away in epic fashion as reality comes crashing back in. My career is over; I'll never play football again.

Since my original injury, I had a feeling it was over, but there was always a thread of hope that *maybe* I'd build my strength back up and be able to still throw the ball. Maybe I wouldn't be Joe Namath, but I could have a career. That's gone now.

Beneath all of the pain and uncertainty, there's also a sliver of relief. The wondering is over; the wait and see is finally finished. Quarterback Paris is dead. I can throw him a funeral and move on with my life.

TRACK 24: SIDE A

Going Home

Benji

I listen outside Paris' door while he cries, trying to decide if I should go in and comfort him or not. When I give in and try the handle, I find it locked, so I decide that must mean he wants to be left alone.

I spend the rest of the night hoping he'll come out of his room, at the very least for something to eat, until I eventually give up and go to bed around two in the morning.

When he emerges from his bedroom in the morning, he's still quiet, and his eyes are a little red and puffy, but he gives me a smile and pulls me in for a kiss.

"Stop looking at me like that; I'm fine."

I want to argue, to tell him again that it's okay to *not* be fine. Sure, he had a feeling his football career was ending, but thinking and knowing are two different things. But there's a sort of desperation in his eyes that makes me think he *needs* to keep telling himself he's okay, at least right now, so I leave it alone.

"I'm not excited about heading back to the snow," I admit with a laugh.

"Same," he agrees. "Maybe I should move back to LA, after all." The comment twists in my chest, reminding me again that as much fun as we have had while we were here, it's over now that we're heading home.

"LA is fun. There are a lot of warm places; you could move to any of them."

"That's true. I'm completely free to live anywhere I want," he says with just a hint of sadness.

After breakfast, we both go back to our rooms to pack, and I call my friend to thank him for letting us borrow the house for the week. Then, I call the driver we've been using all week and arrange a ride to the airport so we can go back to Ohio.

We're both somber as we board the plane a few hours later.

"So…" Paris says, looking out the window of the plane when it starts to taxi down the runway for takeoff. "Are you sticking around a little while or heading back to New York?"

His voice is carefully even, not giving anything away.

"Undecided. We're still doing this fake relationship, right?"

"Yeah, but we don't have to be in the same state to do that."

"True." I try not to sound as disappointed

as I feel.

"Great. We can plan some get togethers for photo ops and do some flirting on Twitter to keep it interesting." His voice still sounds hollow as he makes the suggestion, and I'm not sure if it's because he's feeling the loss like I am or if it has more to do with the other loss he's mourning at the moment.

I told him we both had too much else to worry about right now to think about a relationship, and that's truer now than ever. He needs to rebuild his life, find a new path to his future, and that's going to be a lot easier if he's not worrying about me and my crumbling world at the same time. It's like we're both drowning, and grabbing onto each other isn't going to fix anything; it's only going to drag us both down faster.

Conversation falls off after that, and we decide to put on a movie to pass the long flight home.

Paris

Stepping off the plane in Ohio feels like entering another dimension. The sky is gray, and cold nips at my skin, chasing away the memories of the salty, island air. Benji gets us an Uber from the airport, stopping at my apartment first.

"Are you going back to your parents' house?" I ask.

"For now."

"Will you tell me before you leave again

for New York?" I hope my question doesn't come off as desperate as it feels, but I figure it's better than grabbing onto Benji and begging him not to go.

"I promise."

"Thanks," I say. "And thanks for the trip; it was great."

He gives me a wry smile, eyeing my arm in a sling. "Yeah, you sure owe me one," he replies sarcastically.

"Hey." Using my good hand, I tilt his chin up so he's looking at me. "It was a *great* vacation." I press a brief kiss to his lips before finally climbing out of the backseat of the car and heading into my building, refusing to look back and watch as the car drives away with Benji still in it.

Stepping inside my apartment, I drop my suitcase and close the door behind me. It feels even less like me than it did before I left. I can hear my neighbor through the thin walls, as usual. I see my things scattered about, but it feels too small, too gray, and I'm not sure I can stand to stay here much longer.

Part of me wants to start making plans for the future, to write out a list of places I could move, a checklist of shit I need to get done to wrap up this chapter of my life, to think of all the things I can do now. But a bigger part of me is way too tired to think about any of that. I shuffle to my bedroom, and I'm just about to strip out of my clothes and climb into bed when my phone starts to ring.

My heart leaps, hoping it's Benji telling me he's outside and wants to come up. I feel like a little bit of a dick when I pull it out of my pocket and feel disappointed to see my brother's name on the screen.

"Hey, bro," I answer.

"Hey, you guys home? How was the trip?"

"It was…" *amazing, hot, life changing in too many ways for comfort.* "I hurt my arm again," I say instead of any of the other things popping into my head.

"What?" London sounds panicked. "Is it bad?"

"It's pretty bad," I confirm. "My career is over."

"Holy shit, Paris."

"Yeah. Listen, I'm pretty tired after traveling all day, so I think I'm going to go to bed."

"Are you sure? Can I come over? I'm worried about you."

"I'm fine," I assure him. "I'll talk to you tomorrow."

I hang up and toss my phone onto my nightstand before undressing, with some difficulty due to my sling, and then crawl between the covers, pulling them over my head and closing my eyes.

TRACK 25: SIDE A

It's Not Over

Benji

The day after getting back from the island, I bum around my parents' house for a while, spending time with them and trying to decide what I want to do now. God knows how much longer the band will be on *sabbatical*, if that's what we're still calling it, and I'm not sure what to do with all this free time. Every minute of the last ten years has been on a tight schedule for the record company. Not having anything to do feels all kinds of wrong.

I text with my tattoo artist friend Royal for a while, talking about having him come out to New York to have him ink me soon. I also text with Lando and Cooper until I'm so bored I can hardly see straight and decide to go over to London's.

He answers the door quickly after I knock, looking concerned.

"Oh, hey."

"Wow, what a greeting," I tease, giving him a hug.

"Sorry, I just thought it might be Paris." He waves me inside, and I toe off my shoes, following him to the living room.

"Is Paris supposed to be coming over?" I ask as casually as possible, even as my heart beats a little faster just saying his name.

"He's your boyfriend; shouldn't you know the answer to that?" London jokes.

"You're funny," I say dryly.

"But seriously, I'm a little worried because he sounded really down when I talked to him last night. Maybe it was jet lag or being back in the snow after a week in the tropics, but it made me nervous," he explains. "He told me about his shoulder, and I can only imagine how he must be feeling."

I make a sympathetic noise. "He says he's fine, but there's no way that's true. I think he's doing the best he can to adjust to his new reality, and that might take a little time."

"Yeah," London sighs. "So...you guys totally fucked, right?"

"Ugh," I groan, reaching for one of the decorative pillows on his couch and flinging it at his head. "You seriously need a hobby...or to get laid."

"You offering?" he asks, waggling his eyebrows.

"Sorry, Donnie, not gonna happen."

"And why not?" he presses. "Possibly because you're fucking my brother."

I groan again and can't help laughing at my best friend's persistence. Maybe I should tell him the truth, that we didn't fuck but we did spend the week naked and horny together, swallowing each other's cum and dry humping like wild animals. Okay, I probably shouldn't tell him in that excruciating detail, especially since it's making my dick hard just thinking about it.

"I'll drop it," he says before I can make up my mind about whether to spill the beans or not. "You two looked good together in those pics you shared, and I wouldn't hate having you as my brother-in-law."

I sputter a surprised cough. "Jesus, Donnie. Even if Paris and I *did* fool around, no one has a wedding ring on, that much I can promise you."

"Fine," he sighs. "So, are you going back to New York soon?"

"Not before I kick your ass in *Fortnight*," I say, reaching for the video game controller on his coffee table.

"You're so on."

Paris

Sitting in my apartment feeling sorry for myself, I lay across my couch, looking out the window at the snow falling outside and try to remember the feeling of the heat against my skin, the sand under my feet, the crashing of the ocean waves. It was less than two days ago, but it already feels like a different lifetime.

I lose track of how many times I reach for my phone to text Benji, beg him to come over, ask him to remind me what it was like when we were lost in each other, before the ruins of my life finally crumbled. But we agreed we both had too much going on to start anything, and that's even more true now that it was last week. I need to make plans to go out to California and deal with my agent and the team. I need to figure out what exactly I'm doing with the rest of my life... but all I want is to forget my problems and get lost in Benji a little longer.

The tap at my door is almost too quiet to hear. At first, I assume it's my neighbor making noise, but then it comes again, a little louder the second time. I consider ignoring it. It's more than likely London, and I'm not much in the mood to talk. I know he's going to want to comfort me about my shoulder or try to give me some kind of pep talk about the future. I can't deal with it right now.

"Come on, 'Ris, I know you're home." Benji's voice is muffled through the door, but it has me jumping up off the couch, a smile spreading across my lips for the first time in days. I'm like a school boy with a crush, my heart pounding as I hurry across the living room to open the door.

I pull the door open to find Benji leaning against the doorframe, his arms crossed, his hair pulled back in a messy bun, melting snowflakes in his hair and clinging to his eyelashes.

"What—"

My question is cut off by his lips on mine as he pushes me backward into my apartment, kicking the door closed behind him without breaking the kiss. I grab the back of his neck with my hand that's not in a sling and part my lips to let his tongue in.

"It can still be casual in Ohio, right?" he mumbles against my mouth.

"Mmmhmm."

He walks me backward until the back of my knees hit the couch, and I fall back with an *oomph*.

"Do you have condoms around here?" he asks, looking down at me with a smirk on his kiss swollen lips.

"There's a box on the floor next to my bed." I hadn't bothered to put them away when I unpacked, just tossed them to the floor and called it good enough.

"Be right back."

While he's gone, I unzip my pants and push them off, cursing at the difficulty of doing it with only one hand. I don't bother with my shirt, figuring it'll be more trouble than it's worth with the sling in the way. I can hear Benji's footsteps coming back down the hallway, and I stroke myself slowly, anticipation building in the pit of my stomach until I'm sure I'll drown in it.

Benji steps into back into the living room with condoms and lube in his hand and stops in his tracks, his eyes glued to my hand on my cock. I spread my legs and hold his gaze as I continue to stroke. I've always been right handed, but after the initial recovery after my shoulder surgery, I learned to get along okay with my left hand. Although, right now I'd much rather have what the heat in Benji's eyes is promising me.

"Come here."

He gives himself a little shake and smiles at me before closing the distance between us, tossing the supplies down on the couch cushion beside me, and tugging his shirt over his head. His hair cascades down his bare shoulders as he drops his shirt at my feet. I keep stroking myself as he unbuttons his jeans and slides them down his hips as well.

After seeing him naked all week long, you'd think it would start to lose some of its impact, but it sets my blood on fire all the same. I groan, tightening my grip on my cock.

"I want you inside me," Benji says as he reaches again for the bottle of lube. Another moan falls from my lips, and I have to stop stroking for fear I'm going to bust from his words alone. There's a small voice in the back of my head that tells me this might be a line we can't come back from once we cross it, but I can't find it in me to give a damn right now.

"Do you want to prep me or should I do the

honors?" he asks, uncapping the lube.

"Let me." I release my hold on my cock and hold my hand open so he can squirt the lube onto my fingers, then he climbs onto my lap, straddling me.

His hard cock presses against my stomach while mine gets trapped against his thigh. Benji leans his head down to kiss me, and we both moan when my slicked fingers slide between his ass cheeks and over his hole. His tongue fucks my mouth as I ease one finger inside him, the tight heat of his channel making my cock pulse.

I add a second finger, then a third, stretching him open, taking care to make sure he's ready for me. After my own disastrous first experience bottoming, I've always been sure to take my time.

"I'm ready," Benji says, reaching for the condom and tearing it open before wiggling back a little so he can get to my cock and put it on me. I slowly pull my fingers out of his hole and wipe the leftover lube onto my covered cock.

"This is one of those mid-sex things that you'd better never hold against me, but I feel like I've been waiting for this forever," I confess as I notch the head of my cock against his softened hole.

"God, Paris, you have *no* idea," Benji groans as he lowers himself onto my cock, the tight muscles of his hole squeezing me as he works me inside, bouncing little by little until I'm buried balls deep.

"Fuck, that's so good," I gasp, grabbing onto his ass cheek with my good hand and letting my head loll back against the couch.

Benji leans back, putting his hands against my knees to brace himself, and moans long and low. "Holy fuck, you're so deep inside me," he pants as he rides me, his cock slapping against his stomach with each thrust, the head red and wet with precum.

My lips seek out every bit of his flesh I can reach, kissing his throat, his chest, his peaked nipples, his mouth, memorizing him in yet another new way, even after I spent all week doing just that.

I pull my hand off his ass to wrap it around his cock, and he lets out a strangled cry.

"Yeah, oh god, I'm close," he warns, riding me faster, his eyes rolling back as a blush spreads over his chest and over his face, his channel clamping tighter around me before it starts to flutter and pulse, his cum coating my fingers. I buck my hips up, meeting each of his erratic thrusts as my own release overtakes me, and I see stars.

Benji's thrusts slow, his muscles giving erratic twitches as he presses his face against my shoulder and gives a happy little sigh.

"God damn, that was good," he murmurs.

Too good, I want to agree. If I was hung up on Benji all these years, something tells me this isn't going to do anything to get him out of my system, but I still can't seem to find it in me to care.

"Will you stay?" I ask instead.

"Sure." He presses a kiss to my cheek before climbing off me, wincing and hissing as my softening dick pops out of his ass. I wipe my cum covered hand on my shirt and then take the hand he's offering to help me up.

We head to my bathroom to get cleaned up together, Benji helping me with my shirt and insisting on me taking more pain meds, before we fall into bed and drift off to sleep without another word.

*****

I wake up to find myself alone in bed, and my stomach gives an unhappy twist. I reach for the side of the bed Benji was occupying when I fell asleep and find the sheets cold. I roll over and look at the clock beside my bed—three in the morning. How long has Benji been gone?

I wonder if I'll see him again before he goes back to New York, if he's already on a plane back there. I glance around for my phone before remembering it's probably still in the living room. With a sigh, I heave myself out of bed, shivering when my feet hit the icy hardwood floor.

I shuffle out of my bedroom with a yawn, and I stop dead in my tracks when I see Benji in my living room, standing in front of the window with one of my throw blankets wrapped around his shoulders, his hair seeming to glow in the moonlight.

"I thought you left."

He turns his head and gives me a shy half smile. It's so at odds with the rock star image I see portrayed on his social media accounts, but it's completely in line with the awkward boy I used to know. The one I went to sleep thinking about every night of high school and for too many years after. Just like when I caught him in his glasses on the island. A warm, almost nostalgic feeling blooms in my chest.

"I was going to, but I got lost in thought while I watched the snow," he admits, nodding toward the window. "It's like a living snow globe."

"Oh." I'm not sure what to say. It's not that there isn't anything that *needs* to be said, it's that there's *too much* that I should say, and I'm not sure where to start.

"Want to sit and watch it together for a little while?" he offers, and I nod, happy for an excuse to sit down on the couch and pat my lap. He climbs on, careful of my bad shoulder, and wraps the blanket around both of us. His skin is still warm as he settles into my lap, his hair tickling my skin as he rests his head against my shoulder, and we both look out the window to watch large snowflakes fall.

"I'm probably going to LA this weekend,"

I say eventually. "I need to meet with my agent and the coach."

"And look for an apartment out there?" he asks, likely remembering our conversation on the plane.

"I'm not sure. I don't know what I want. I feel so turned around; it's hard to figure out which way is up."

"I get that," he assures me. "I was thinking about going back to New York tomorrow."

"Right." I tighten my hand against his hip, biting my tongue against asking him to come with me to LA or to stay here in Ohio and wait for me to get back. It's too soon to say goodbye.

"It's not goodbye, 'Ris," he says as if he can read my thoughts.

"I know," I lie.

We fall quiet again after that, and the snow continues to fall. Eventually, Benji's weight relaxes against me, and I tilt my head to find him fast asleep, his head against my shoulder.

If I had the use of both arms, I'd carry him back to bed, but that's certainly not going to happen one handed. So, I sit and continue to stare out the window, imagining a future without football. Every single one that comes to mind seems to have Benji in it, and I curse myself for getting into this position to start falling for a man who doesn't seem the least bit interested in being tied down to anyone or anything.

At some point I fall asleep too, and when I wake up, morning sun is streaming through the windows, bright as it reflects off the snow outside. Benji is gone, and there's a note on my coffee table. I pull the blankets tighter around my shoulders before reaching for the note.

Dear Boyfriend,

I'm leaving on a jet plane...lol. I hope all goes well in LA, call me, video chat me, keep in touch! And come out to New York to see me soon, pretty please? I bet we can find a lot of fun ways to be casual in New York too ;) . Give London a hug for me and take care of yourself.

Love,
Benji

I choke up a little at the sign off. I'm sure he means it in the same way he tells London he loves him. We're friends, closer friends than we've ever been. And as much as I'd love to jump on a plane and follow him to New York right now, I need to get my ass to the other side of the country and start wrapping up my old life so I can start a new one.

TRACK 26: SIDE A

Lost in LA

Benji

All I can think about on the flight back to New York is leaving Paris behind. But I'm not leaving him behind, not really. I'm giving him space to sort his life out, and I need to do the same.

I look around at my penthouse full of *stuff,* and for the first time, I can relate to Jude's tendency to rage through his own place demolishing everything in sight. I bet there's something cathartic about that kind of destruction.

I consider calling Lando to check in or going out to the club to lose myself in a sea of people, but I end up sitting down at my piano and bleeding everything from the past few weeks, all the beauty and uncertainty and joy into music, which is the best therapy I can think of.

I bang on my keyboard; I mess around with my violin. I jot down random melodies. I stand in front of my floor to ceiling windows watching snow fall and missing Ohio...or at least someone I left in Ohio. And when I can't take the silence of my place a second longer, I call Cooper.

"Hey man, you still on that island you've been posting about?" he asks as soon as he answers.

"I wish," I chuckle. "Currently sitting in my place in New York watching the snow come down."

"I feel for you. I'm doing the same in Vermont right now," he says. "How were your holidays? Looked like you found someone interesting to spend time with."

A smile spreads across my lips, my chest warming as I think of Paris again. Part of me is still sure that whole vacation was some sort of wild dream. I didn't really have sex with the man I've been crushing on practically my entire life, right?

"Yeah, it was amazing," I answer, reluctant to give details. I want to horde them all to myself.

"That's great. I, uh, ended up spending some time with Orion," he confesses, and I perk up.

Cooper and Orion's falling out was a huge deal in the music world a few years back. Rumors flew everywhere when they canceled a tour, and Orion, the lead guitarist for Last Weekend, basically vanished off the face of the earth. The band has been in limbo ever since, refusing to say they've broken up, but remaining tight lipped about what happened and whether they'd ever record or tour again. When their contract with Epic came up for renewal last year, they didn't re-sign. The label even offered to sign Cooper as a solo artist instead, but he refused, saying it was his band or nothing at all.

"Holy shit, how's he doing?"

Our very first tour was opening for Last Weekend. Orion and I had gotten along great. I can't imagine anyone meeting him and not liking him. It was clear he was wrestling his own demons, much like Lincoln and Jude, but there was a quiet sweetness about him that drew me in.

"I think he's doing well. He seems better than I've ever seen him, honestly." There's a hint of sadness in Coopers voice that makes me wonder about his relationship with his guitarist. When the band was making headlines and topping charts, there was constant speculation about whether the two of them were more than friends. They were beyond close, almost joined at the hip, and when Orion pulled a vanishing act Cooper was a mess.

"That's good to hear. Do you think the band will sign with Epic again and get back to recording?"

Cooper sighs. "I don't see us going back to Epic. Part of the issue is that they worked us into the ground, demanding a schedule that destroyed us."

I make a sympathetic noise. He's not wrong. I have no doubt that part of our issue is the insane touring schedule Epic keeps us on. Yes, Lincoln and Jude are a mess, but not having any time to rest is only making matters worse.

"Maybe another label then?"

"Maybe," he echoes, not sounding so sure of it himself.

Cooper's defeated tone twists in my gut like a knife. Will I be in his same position soon? A musician without a band is a sad sight to see.

"I'm sure you guys will figure things out."

"I sure as hell hope so."

Paris

The meetings with my agent and the coach of the team go about as well as could be expected, which is to say neither were happy, and it was about as much fun as going to the dentist. With it being off season, at least I don't have to meet with the team. Some of them were good guys, but for the most part, I'm sure they'll all be thrilled to hear the news.

My agent schedules a press conference for a few days from now, so I agree to stay in town until it's done. And then she tells me about all the possibilities for my career going forward, like sportscasting. I tell her I'll consider it and then get the hell out of her office as fast as I can.

It's been five days since Benji went home

to New York, and we've exchanged a few texts here and there, but I've been a little too busy wallowing to offer much more than that. With these meetings over with, I feel like a weight has been lifted. I still have no clue what my future looks like necessarily, but at least I'm free to move forward and find out now.

I stop outside a cafe and sit down at one of the tables on the sidewalk, pulling out my phone to call Benji.

"How'd it go?" he asks as soon as he answers.

"Meh, you know."

"Are you doing okay?"

"Better than I expected, honestly. It's kind of a relief," I admit. "How have you been? How's New York treating you?"

"Cold," he grumbles, and I laugh. "I finally got word that Lincoln is going to be back in New York early next month, and we're going to schedule a band meeting for the end of the month."

"Are you nervous about it?"

"Yeah," he says. "I think the waiting and not knowing is the worst part, though."

"I can totally relate. Whatever happens, you'll find a new way forward. You're the most talented musician I've ever known, and you're going to find a way to bring music to the world."

"Thank you, I needed to hear that."

"You're welcome."

"So, I was wondering—" Before Benji can finish telling me what exactly he's wondering, a shadow falls over me, and I look up to see Elliot standing in front of me looking surprised and assessing.

"Hey, can I call you back later?"

"Oh, yeah sure."

"Sorry, my ex seems to have found me," I tell him in case a paparazzi happens by and takes a picture of us together.

"*Oh*," Benji says again. "Yeah, go ahead, call whenever. Good luck."

"Thanks, bye." I hang up and pocket my phone. "Can I help you with something, or are you just here to block out my sun?"

"Don't be grouchy. I'm as surprised as you are to find you in LA. I thought you were in Michigan."

"Ohio," I correct, rolling my eyes. As if he didn't come running out to Ohio to try to win me back a few weeks ago. I have an intense moment of wondering what I ever saw in him.

"Whatever." He waves it off. "Mind if I sit? I think we have some catching up to do."

"Fine," I agree with a sigh. This is just another step in closing that chapter of my life, so I might as well get it over with. "How's the boyfriend?" I ask as soon as he sits down.

"Busy with the season coming up," he admits with a shrug. "Just like you always were."

"Yeah, you date an athlete that's going to

happen."

Elliot frowns. "I'm sorry I hurt your feelings."

"My feelings are fine. It sucked hearing you were cheating on me, but things were already over anyway; I'm over it."

"Because you're with Benji now?" he asks bitterly.

"No, because our relationship wasn't working, and it's better that it's over now. Me being with Benji is a completely separate entity to whatever you and I used to have." As I say it, I know it's true. I know Benji thought I suggested the fake relationship to get back at my ex, but I was a lot more interested in getting the focus off my career than anything else. Making Elliot jealous is a nice little bonus, but honestly, it's not the end goal.

"You two are really together then?" he pries.

"I don't think it's any of your business anymore," I answer. "We had what we had, and that's over now. You're with someone else, I'm moving on; let's put the past in the past."

"We were good together," he says, reaching for my hand.

"No, we really weren't. We had some good times, but at the end of the day, what we had was shallow."

His frown deepens, and his face goes a little red. I wouldn't say it to his face, but everything about Elliot is shallow. There are a lot of things he and Benji have in common—their tendency to constantly seek validation from others, their love of showing off their success, but that's all there is to Elliot. Beneath the surface, Benji is so much more.

"I hope this helped with closure, El. I truly wish you a good life."

He gets up without another word and storms away, and even more of the weight of my former life lifts.

TRACK 27: SIDE A
Drunk Dial

Benji

I smile as I read Paris' recent Tweet. *@BenjiCasparian reminds me of the island;)* followed by a photo of a bottle of tequila. I like it, and Tweet back at him.

It's been two weeks since I got back to New York and Paris officially left his team. The press conference was a little painful to watch, not because he wasn't charismatic as hell answering all the questions they flung at him, but because the sadness in his eyes was obvious. I called him afterward to make sure he was okay, and he assured me over and over that he was until he decided to take a different tactic and distracted me with phone sex.

I don't for a second believe he's totally fine with how things turned out, but I think he wants to be, and that he will be, so I've decided not to push him to talk any more about it. He has a right to take his time to grieve, and he has a right to move on in whatever timeframe he chooses.

He's been sending me photos all week as

he packs up his apartment, telling me over and over how slow going it is to do one handed, but not outright asking me to come back and help him, even though every once in a while, I get the sense it's what he's hinting at. He has to wear the sling another week, and then he can get back to physical therapy, starting from square one with no hope of building up to throwing a football again.

I've considered taking it upon myself to go back out to Ohio to see him again even without an invitation, but it feels like it's overstepping. We haven't brought up where things stand again, as far as being casual or if we'll hook up again, but we *have* had some very *stimulating* video chats.

Switching from Twitter to text, I send a message to Paris.

Benji: How's the packing going?
Paris: Nearly done! Just signed a six-month lease on an apartment in Chicago, and the movers will be here tomorrow.
Benji: That's great! But you DO know it snows in Chicago, right?
Paris: Oh shit, better change my plans
Benji: lol
Paris: I'm still trying to figure out what I'm going to do, so I figured I'd start by getting back to civilization and going from there. Chicago always seemed like a cool city, I fig-

ured what the hell
Benji: Not as good as New York ;)
Paris: New York isn't off the table...

My heart flutters, wondering at the implication. Does he just mean he's considering New York in general or that it's contingent on a theoretical relationship we might have? I may tease, but there's no way I'd push him to make the move here right now. He's trying to figure out what his life looks like right now, and I need to give him the space to do that.

Paris: Any wild plans for the weekend?
Benji: Flying out my tattoo guy and his boyfriends to give me some fresh ink.
Paris: Send pics when it's done

A blush creeps into my cheeks, even though he can't see me. I wonder what he'll think about the tattoo I'm having Royal give me.

Benji: I've gotta run, but talk later
Paris: Later

I shove my phone back into my pocket and get ready to go to the airport to pick up Royal and his boyfriends. I could've sent a driver, but I thought it would be more fun to do it myself. I grab my handmade sign that reads *Porn Conven-*

tion to hold at the airport and head out.

The airport is crazy busy, and I get stopped a number of times to ask for a selfie. It seems like our plan is working, because it's certainly more attention than I normally get when I'm out without the rest of the band.

When I spot my tattoo artist, Royal, I hold up the sign I made so he can see it. His eyes zero in, and an amused smile spreads across his lips. He gestures to the two men with him to follow as he makes his way over to me.

"You know, you really shouldn't tease about porn conventions; now, I want to go to one," he says when he reaches me.

I chuckle and pull him into a hug. We met last year when Downward Spiral had a secret show in Las Vegas. I spotted a group of people in the crowd with the most killer tattoos I'd ever seen. After the show, I had security bring them back stage so I could ask who did their work, and it turned out they were all tattoo artists in Seattle. Royal and I struck up a friendship, messaging regularly since then. Lando texted me last week asking me for a recommendation for a tattoo artist, and I told him if he wanted ink, we'd make sure he got the best. It's a win-win since I've been itching for some new ink myself.

"You remember Nash and Zade from Las Vegas?" He introduces his men, and yes, I do remember them from Vegas, and I've certainly heard a lot about them since I've been talking to Royal. He may be a little wild with a wicked sense of humor, but he's also head over heels for his boyfriends, talking about them constantly.

"I'm glad you guys were all able to make it." I give each of them a hug as well. "I figured you'd want your privacy, so I booked you a room at the Hilton."

"Swanky," Zade says with a smile. "Hotel sex is the best, isn't it?" he asks his boyfriends. Royal nods emphatically, and Nash blushes a little and rolls his eyes.

"I'll drop you off at the hotel so you can settle in, shower, fuck, whatever, and then Royal, I'll leave you with my driver so you can come over to do my tattoo whenever you're up for it."

*****

Royal shows up at my place a few hours later with all the things he needs to do my ink.

"How's the hotel?" I ask as I wave him inside.

"Fucking amazing. Zade and Nash were planning to try out the Jacuzzi tub when I left."

"Is that weird?" I ask with interest.

"Having two boyfriends who are back at the hotel fucking right now?" Royal clarifies with a smirk.

"Yeah, that."

"Nah, it's hot as hell."

"I can't even handle one man in my life, let

alone two," I joke.

"Seems you're doing okay with that football player so far."

"Are you Instagram stalking me?" I tease.

"Duh. It's not like I get to be besties with a ton of celebrities; it's cool as fuck," he says. "Now, what am I doing for your ink today?"

I grab my tablet off the table and pull up a photo of red hibiscus flowers to show him. "I want these, covering my back."

"Flowers, cool." He studies the image for a second and then grabs his notebook to work on a sketch. The process of getting a tattoo is soothing. He takes his time using transfer paper to cover my back with rough sketches of the flowers and then sets up his ink and equipment.

When the buzzing needle pierces my skin for the first time, I sigh and relax into the familiar feeling. I close my eyes and get comfortable, knowing this is going to take at least a few hours.

We laugh and chat while he works. We don't get into anything too deep or earth shattering, but it's exactly what I need.

After he finishes my ink, I offer to show Royal some of my instruments. Leading him to my music studio, I grab my sitar down off the wall and make myself comfortable on the floor to play it, while Royal watches with interest.

"Why do I get the feeling you can play literally anything?" he says as I find a way to play some vague Taylor Swift melodies with the instrument.

"Instruments I can do, but you do *not* want to hear me sing. I sound like a cat being swung around in a sack."

Royal chuckles. "Now I *really* want to hear it."

I hear the sound of my front door opening. My doorman has the go-head to let any of the guys in if they ever show up, so I assume it's Lando here for his tattoo.

"Lando, get your ass in here. I need vocals," I call out, and I hear him chuckle.

A minute later, he appears in the doorway with another man in tow. I eye his man, curly brown hair covered by a beanie, a shy smile with dimples on his cheeks, ink peeking out from under his sleeves. I definitely approve.

Royal and Lando make introductions. They met in Vegas too, of course, but haven't talked since.

"And this is Dawson," Lando introduces the man with him.

Dawson...it takes me a second to place the name, and when it clicks, I smile.

"*Finally*, you can stop moping around about this guy."

Lando's eyes go wide, and he turns to face Dawson before saying, "I wasn't moping."

Rather than answering out loud, the man responds in sign language. Lando looks happier than I've seen him in a decade, and for the first time, a flicker of hope about the future of the band settles in my chest. I heard from Archer that Lincoln got back together with his ex over Christmas, Jude is supposedly off drugs, and apparently Lando found his muse. Maybe we're not doomed after all.

"Look what I had Royal do for me this morning before you got here," I say, standing up and pulling my shirt off to show him

"Wow, that's incredible. I'm just glad you got some serious work done because I was feeling really silly about you flying him across the country just so I could get a quote done."

"Even if it was just the quote, you wouldn't hear me complaining. Having Benji fly me and my partners out on a private flight for the weekend...this is kick ass."

We make small talk a few more minutes before Royal suggests we head out to the living room so he can get set up again for Lando's tattoo. While Royal sets up, Lando and Dawson make eyes at each other and a deep longing settles over me. I know Paris needs space to get his life figured out, but fuck if I don't miss him already.

Since Lando is only getting a quote, Royal gets it done in no time at all.

"Hey, can Dawson teach me some swear words in sign language?" Royal asks.

Dawson nods eagerly and shows Royal what I assume are going to become his new favorite hand gestures.

"We're thinking about heading out to the club later if you guys want to join," I offer.

"We'll think about it," Lando says, but I can tell by the way they're looking at each other that they'll likely go back to Lando's place and spend the rest of the evening in bed. Lucky bastards.

"So, you want to go get drunk?" I offer once Lando's gone.

"Abso-fucking-loutely," he agrees with a smirk.

"Good, call your men and tell them we're on our way to pick them up."

I lead them into the VIP section when we get to the club, and their excitement is better than all the alcohol in the world, although there *is* also alcohol. I order us a bottle of expensive whiskey while Royal and Zade decide to go dance, leaving me with Nash.

"Those two seem like a handful," I say, nodding at his men, grinding on each other shamelessly at the edge of the dance floor.

"They are, but they're worth it."

"That must be nice," I sigh, my mind wandering back to Paris again. It's only been a few weeks; I shouldn't miss him this much.

"You're dating a football player, right? Sorry, I don't follow sports, so I have no idea who he is."

I thank the waitress and give her a big

tip when she brings over the whiskey, pouring a glass for each of us.

"Can you keep a secret?" I ask Nash.

"Sure."

"It's just for publicity."

"Oh, really? I always wondered if that was a thing. Is it common?"

I shrug. "Straight up pretending to date isn't very common, but dating someone for the press is *way* more common than you'd think among the rich and fabulous."

"That's crazy. So, you and Paris are friends or what?"

I smile, taking a sip of my drink. "We've been friends forever. We lost contact for a long time, but I'm really glad to have him back in my life again."

"Are you sure the relationship is fake?" he asks with humor in his voice.

"Unfortunately. I mean, we're fooling around too, but we're too busy for anything more."

"Mmm." He takes a sip of his own drink, his eyes on me too perceptive, making me squirm. "Life's too short to be too busy for love."

I bark out an uncomfortable laugh. "Whoa, who said anything about love?"

Nash shrugs and takes another sip of his drink while I down mine in one gulp before pouring myself a second glass. Royal and Zade return and drag Nash onto the dance floor. They try to cajole me too, but I'm more than happy to sit and enjoy my drink.

Two drinks turns into three, and before I know it, half the bottle is gone, and Nash's words about life being too short seem to be the most significant thing I've ever heard.

I pull my phone out of my pocket and dial Paris.

"Hey, whoa, it's loud there," he says when he answers.

"Yeah, out at the club."

"That sounds fun."

"It'd be more fun if you were here," I slur flirtatiously.

"Oh yeah?"

"Yeah, you should come to New York," I say. "I-I miss you."

Paris is quiet on the other end for a few heart beats, and I curse myself for coming on too strong. I told him this was casual, and a few drinks later, I'm calling and saying shit like I miss him, even if it *is* true.

"I'll see what I can do. Now, get back to your fun with your tattoo friends."

"Okay. But you really should come," I insist one last time.

Paris chuckles; the sound is so warm I want to curl up inside it and live there.

"Get home safe when the fun is over," he says rather than responding to my actual request. "Night, Benji."

TRACK 28: SIDE A

I'll be There

Paris

Getting on a plane to New York after Benji's phone call seemed reasonable until I found myself standing at JFK airport with no idea where Benji lives and feeling a little embarrassed about the call I'm going to have to make.

"Yeah?" Benji grunts a greeting after the fifth ring.

"Morning, sunshine. Hungover?"

"I'm dying," he complains.

"Poor baby," I tease with a laugh.

"Did you just call to make fun of me? Because if so, I'm hanging up."

"Actually," I clear my throat. "I called to ask for your address."

"Why do you need my address?" he asks with a yawn.

"Uber drivers like to have them. They get super pissed if you ask them to just drive you around the city hoping to spot someone," I joke.

"What?" That seems to wake him up. "You're here? You're in the city?"

"Standing in the airport as we speak."

"Holy shit. Hold on, I'll come pick you up." I hear rustling on his end followed by cursing. I can picture him stumbling out of bed half awake and looking a mess.

"You don't have to do that. Give me your address, and I'll be there soon; you won't even have to get dressed. In fact, I'd prefer if you weren't."

"Now *that's* tempting." He rattles off his address for me, and I promise to be there soon.

I meet my Uber outside and ask him to make a stop so I can pick up coffee on the way to Benji's.

His building is swanky as hell, which doesn't come as much of a surprise. I'm greeted by a doorman who tells me Benji already called down about my arrival and has to key a code into the elevator so it'll take me to his floor.

My stomach flutters with excitement as I ride the elevator up to his floor. When he called last night and told me he wanted me to come visit, it sounded like there was so much more there than a simple invitation. Maybe I'm reading too much into it or putting my own spin on what he said, but whatever the case, I can't wait to see him again.

The doors ding and slide open into a hallway with only one door. With coffee in one hand and my sling on the other, I use my foot to knock at the door. It swings open, and Benji is gloriously naked on the other side.

"God damn, it's good to see you." He grabs the back of my neck and drags me into a kiss, nearly making me drop the coffee. But as his tongue invades my mouth, his lips sweet and hot against mine, I couldn't give less of a shit about the coffee.

"I can't believe you're here," he mumbles against my lips.

I smile with relief and kiss him deeper. His tongue is minty as it licks inside my mouth, his naked body rubbing against mine as his hands roam shamelessly over me, grinding his hard cock against my thigh. If I didn't have one hand in a sling and the other holding coffee, I'd grab his ass and haul him into my arms.

"Wait, aren't you supposed to be moving to Chicago today?" he asks, pulling back and scrunching up his eyebrows.

"Not like I was going to be the one doing any of the heavy lifting," I say, nodding toward my bad shoulder. "Everything was packed, and I had the movers scheduled, all I had to do was give them the address and a key, and I was free to spend the weekend here instead."

"In that case, put the coffee down and come to bed."

He spins around, and I watch with interest as his ass flexes with each step down the hallway. I catch only a quick glimpse of the new, bright red tattoo covering his back, but before I can tell exactly what it is, he's rounding the corner out of sight.

I glance around, taking in his place for the first time. It almost looks like a museum with art covering the walls, along with African masks, various instruments, and things I can't even place. I spot the things he bought when we were on the island, and my chest warms at the memories.

I spot a little table that has mail and a set of keys on it, next to the door, but I'm afraid it's some sort of priceless artifact, so I head down the hall in search of the kitchen to put the coffee down, dropping my duffle bag of clothes on the floor beside it.

When I find my way to his bedroom, he's spread out on the bed waiting for me.

"Took you long enough," he complains.

"You should've given me a map of this place if you didn't want me to get lost."

He ignores my comment, instead smiling and crooking a finger at me. "Come kiss me."

I definitely don't need to be asked twice. Climbing onto the bed, I hover over Benji, putting all my weight on my good arm, getting drunk on the way his body unconsciously arches up to meet mine as soon as our lips meet. I could drown in his taste, the sounds he makes, the feeling of him against me and under me.

"I want you inside me," he moans into my mouth.

"Condoms?"

"Nightstand drawer," he answers while making quick work of getting my pants open. Since I still only have one good arm, once I grab the supplies out of the drawer, I roll onto my back, and Benji straddles me.

He preps himself hurriedly while I suit up, and then he's sliding down onto my cock. He winces as my cock stretches him, but doesn't stop, just rocks his hips, slowly taking me in inch by inch until I'm fully buried inside the tight heat of his ass.

He throws his head back and moans. I lose track of time and myself as Benji rides me. My world focuses in on Benji, and everything else becomes a blur of sweat slicked bodies, the sound of slapping skin, the salty taste of his skin under my tongue, goosebumps rising on his flesh just before his pupils dilate, and his muscles tense. He comes without a hand on his cock, the rhythmic pulsing of his channel milking my own orgasm from me in a wave of heat and stars in my vision.

It's incredible and heady and fucking addictive.

Benji climbs off me and rolls onto his back beside me while I take off the used condom and glance around for somewhere to toss it.

"The floor is fine for now," he assures me with a yawn.

I toss it on the floor like he says to and then

roll back and hold open my good arm for him to rest his head on my shoulder.

"So, I take it you're glad I came?"

"Very glad," Benji assures me. "I was a little worried I made an ass of myself calling you last night."

"It was nice to know you missed me," I confess. "I know this is casual, but I *do* like you, Benji."

He smiles and shuffles as close as possible, his entire body plastered against mine. "I kind of like you too, 'Ris."

We lay in silence for a while, dozing on and off between random bouts of conversation. We talk about what's been going on in our lives the past few weeks, about random pointless topics, and about our past—reminiscing about our teenage years. The only thing we completely avoid talking about is the future.

"How are you doing with your shoulder, by the way?" he asks.

I know he doesn't mean physically.

"Better than I expected," I admit. "I think I did most of my mourning last year, after my surgery. I didn't expect to hurt my shoulder a second time, but I was already emotionally resigning myself to the fact that I likely wouldn't play again. In a way, it's a relief to have it done and over with. Waiting to find out what would happen was the hardest part."

"I can relate," Benji agrees with a sigh before we return to lighter topics again for a long while.

"I have to pee," Benji says reluctantly sometime in the early afternoon, rolling out of my arms and sitting up. He scoots to the edge of the bed to get up, and I notice the new tattoo taking up his entire back again, and this time I'm close enough to get a good look at it. It's bright red and looks like flowers. The possible meaning of it hits me in the chest, and I sit up to get a better look.

"Are these hibiscus flowers?"

He turns his head and gives me a shy smile over his shoulder. "Yes."

"Benji, I—"

He cuts me off with a kiss. "Our lives are a mess, 'Ris; let's not make it more complicated."

"Right," I agree.

As he walks out of the room, I feel a mixture of relief that I'm not alone in feeling more than I should and disappointed. I know he's right; everything with his band is still up in the air. Neither of us know where we'll live or what career we'll have in six months; it's the completely wrong time to start something more. But maybe one day...

I hear the muffled sound of my phone ringing from somewhere. I sit up and look around for my pants, spotting them near the foot of the bed. It's a video call from London, and I don't think twice before hitting to accept the call.

"Hey, bro, I was—" he starts, cutting himself off as his gaze drift behind me. "Are you at Benji's?"

Damn.

"Um…" I consider if there's a lie that could get me out of this, but decide there isn't one. And honestly, I'd rather not flat out lie to London. "Yeah, I am. I flew out to New York this morning."

"I fucking *knew* you two were hooking up."

Benji walks back into the room, stopping in his tracks when he realizes London's on the phone.

"Is that Benji?" my brother asks. "Tell him to get the fuck over here so I can yell at him."

Benji rolls his eyes and climbs back onto the bed to stick his face into the frame of the video.

"Hey, I'm having sex with your brother," Benji says casually. "Don't make a big deal out of it, okay?"

"Don't make a big deal out of it? Are you insane?" he asks. "This is *huge*. Also, you owe me a thousand bucks."

"No, it's not. That's why we didn't tell you. And I'll Paypal you the money once I have pants on."

"What do you mean it's not huge?" London frowns.

"We're both trying to pick up the pieces of our broken lives; the last thing we need right now is the complication of a relationship."

"Whatever you two need to tell your-selves." London snorts a laugh and rolls his eyes. "I *was* calling to ask if you needed any help with the move today, but I guess that would be a no. Give me a call whenever."

"Will do. Later, bro."

"Love you, Donnie," Benji says, blowing a kiss at him before we disconnect. A little niggle of jealousy worms its way into my chest, but I do my best to push it away.

"I should call my tattoo artist, Royal, and see if they want to meet for lunch or anything. They're in town until tomorrow."

"Sounds good."

Benji

I'd feel bad about staying in bed with Paris way past noon if Royal didn't sound tired and happy when I called. They seem to be enjoying themselves just fine, so I don't bother to make apologies. They agree to meet for lunch so we both get showered and dressed so we're present-able to go out in public.

The place we're meeting isn't far, so we de-cide to walk, even though it's fairly cold out. Our breath fogs the air, my nose freezing almost in-stantly. I pull my scarf a little tighter around me and reach for Paris' gloved hand, holding it with mine.

We cut through Central Park, and I imagine coming back here in the summer with him when it's nice out. Maybe we could have a picnic. Would that be completely lame? I smile at the thought of feeding Paris a strawberry while we're laying on a blanket in the grass, and I decide even if it's lame, I'd really like to do it.

Feeling playful, I let go of his hand and stoop to pick up a handful of snow. When Paris' back is to me, I hurriedly form it into a makeshift ball and aim it right at the back of his head.

"Hey," he yelps, and I double over laughing. "Fuck, that's cold! It's all down my coat," he complains while I start making another snowball.

"Do something about it," I challenge.

He stoops down. Using his left hand, he struggles to make his own snowball before I hurl another one at him.

"You shouldn't pick on the handicapped," he grumbles.

"Oh please, like you won't be murdering me with snowballs if your arm was in working order."

He manages to get a couple of hits in while I laugh and try to throw another one that he manages to dodge before coming at me and grabbing me around the waist to kiss me. I smile against his ice cold lips and when we part, I notice someone filming our whole exchange.

"Free publicity?" I say, nodding in the direction of the guy and then giving him a friendly wave. His eyes go wide, and he stops filming.

"Good, give everyone something to talk about other than the untimely end of my football career," he grumbles. "Ever since the press conference a couple of weeks ago, it's been nonstop with questions on social media, reporters calling to ask stupid questions like how do I feel about my career ending and what I'm planning to do now. Maybe we should have sex out here in Central Park; *that* should give them something to talk about."

"I'm game if you are," I joke, taking his hand again and continuing our walk.

Lunch with Royal and his partners is great, but I could've done without all the knowing looks from Nash when I introduced them to Paris. They assure me they're having no problem entertaining themselves in New York, so I put any bit of worry aside about needing to entertain them now that Paris is here.

After lunch, I call a car to take them back to their hotel and Paris and me back to my place to make the most of the weekend before he has to go home to Chicago.

*****

As soon as we get back to my place after lunch, we can hardly keep our hands off each other long enough to make it to my bedroom. Our mouths crash together, our hands fumbling as I drag him onto the bed on top of me, both of us clumsily undressing as our tongues tangle and slide against each other. Paris scrapes his teeth against my jaw, drawing a shiver and a whimper from me. It's all I can do to get naked so I can feel him against me.

"I want you so much," I murmur against his lips as I work his pants open and shove them down his hips as far as I can reach before he has to take over and finish getting them off while I do the same with my own. I hiss as he drags my shirt up, my skin still tender from my fresh tattoo.

"Are you okay?" Paris checks.

"Yeah, sorry, tattoo is still sore. I'll be fine." I push him back and climb on top of him, thrusting my erection against his, making us both groan.

"I can't get enough of you. I thought it was something about the island—the water or the sun or the tequila—but I think it's just you, Benji."

His words make me whimper. They're almost too good to be true. I reach between us and wrap my hand around both our cocks, slowly stroking them, feeling our tips grow slick with precum and using my thumb to mix our fluids together. Paris licks and sucks my throat, no doubt leaving bruises and love marks that I'll wear for days to come. The thought sends a thrill through me and my cock jerks against his.

"I want you inside me again."

He moans in approval and I reach over to

grab the supplies from the nightstand where he left them earlier.

Still stretched from earlier, it doesn't take long to get myself prepped. My hole is a little tender, but nothing unbearable, although there's a strong chance I'll be singing a different tune later, but I'll happily take it.

"Ready?" Paris asks when I pull my fingers out of my hole and wipe the excess lube on my bedspread. By the end of the weekend my bed is going to be covered in all manner of cum and lube, but the extra load of laundry I'll have to do will be more than worth it.

"So ready," I assure him lining his cock up with my hole.. My cock flexes and drips at the sight of his gorgeous, muscular body between my legs, the head of his cock rubbing against my entrance as he smiles up at me with a teasing glint in his eye.

I gasp as he bucks his hips up and pushes inside, a slight twinge of pain making me tense before the pleasure of him slowly filling me takes over. He rocks his hips gently, taking his time as he leans up to kiss me. When his hips are flush with the back of my thighs, he stills, pressing his face into my throat and breathing in deeply. My heart flutters, and my breath catches at the tenderness of the moment, his lips ghosting against my skin, our bodies fully connected.

When he finally pulls out and thrusts back in, it's not a frenzied fuck like we shared earlier;

it's slow and deliberate.

"Did you know I used to dream of this?" Paris whispers against my ear as he moves he holds my hips and moves me on his cock in deep, measured thrusts that make my head swim and my body ache for more. "I had such a crush on you, and I felt like such an asshole because I thought you were London's."

I groan in response, unable to form a coherent response with the length of his cock pressing against my prostate with every torturous thrust. I want to tell him I had a crush on him too, for *so* fucking long. That I was in over my head the minute I laid eyes on him. I want to tell him I don't think I'll ever be able to let him go now that I've had him. It's probably a good thing his cock is making me too stupid to talk because I might say something neither of us is ready for.

"So good," I pant as he fucks me so deep, I swear I can feel it in the pit of my stomach. "God, Paris," I moan and dig my fingers into his arms, rocking into every one of his thrusts.

"Say it again," he begs. "Say my name."

"Paris," I whimper as heat starts to pool in the pit of my stomach, his cock making me feel so fucking full, his body feeling like heaven everywhere we touch. "Paris," I whisper again as my erection drags against his hard stomach, leaving his abs and hair sticky with precum. "Paris," I pant, gripping his bicep like it's the only thing keeping me anchored to the earth.

"Paris," I cry as pleasure washes over me, my balls constricting, my toes curling, my eyes rolling back as I come in long, slow waves that seem to go on and on forever.

"Benji," he moans my name, and I can feel his answering pulses deep inside me as he follows me over the edge.

*****

Paris is fast asleep when my doorman calls my cell phone.

"What's up?"

"Sir, Jude is here to see you. I know you have a guest. Should I tell him to come back another time?"

"*Jude* is here?" I repeat in complete shock.

"Yes, sir."

I had no idea Jude was even back in town. I know Lando is, and Lincoln came and went, but as far as I knew, Jude was still on the West Coast with Archer and the drug counselor. Why Jude would be here to see me, I couldn't begin to guess.

"Um, go ahead and send him up."

"Will do."

I slide out of bed, careful not to wake Paris. I slip into some clothes and go to open the door for Jude.

"I thought my doorman was huffing paint when he said you were here to see me," I joke when I see Jude standing in the hallway looking contrite and peaceful in a way I've never seen him. Even before he picked up the drug habit on our first tour, there was always a chaos about his personality. He had a rough home life, like Lincoln did. Lando and I never quite knew how to relate to them in that aspect, so we tried to pretend it didn't exist. But now, there's a calmness about him.

I step aside to let Jude inside.

"He said you had someone here; I hope I'm not interrupting anything?"

"Nothing that can't wait. You want a drink or anything?"

"Just some water?" he asks, and I nearly stumble over my own feet in surprise. Coke is Jude's drug of choice, but I've *never* seen him turn down a drink...or ten before.

"Coming right up. Have a seat." I gesture toward the living room and then head into the kitchen to grab a couple of water bottles.

"So, where's the *guest*?" Jude asks when I return to the living room. The way he's saying *guest,* I have to guess he's been off social media during his break and has no idea I'm supposed to be dating Paris.

"Oh, he's in the bedroom, but he's a bit *tied up* at the moment," I answer with a wink, and Jude snorts into his water bottle.

"Damn, I didn't know you were into bondage."

I shrug. I'm not sure why I lied and pretended there was something kinky going on in my bedroom instead of Paris sound asleep. My head is still a little fucked up from how intense the sex was when we got home earlier. Maybe it's just easier to pretend it's nothing but a kinky fuck than to face what might really be happening between us. Maybe if I pretend to others that what Paris and I have is purely sexual, I'll believe it too, at least for a little while.

"So, who's the guy?"

"The guy is...not what you came here to talk about. What's up?"

"I tried to stop by Lincoln's, but he's out of town again."

"Oh, so I'm second choice? Thanks," I tease, my curiosity growing.

"I didn't mean it like that. I just..." He takes another sip of water, his knee bouncing and his shoulders tense. I sit quietly, giving him a chance to gather his thoughts and say whatever he came here to say. "I've done nothing but cause trouble for the band over the past ten years, and I had to apologize to someone. I had to find out if it's too late for me to make things right and regain your trust."

I'm sure surprise is written all over my face as I put my hand on his shoulder.

"Oh, Jude. It's not too late. We may have lost our way, but the four of us are brothers, and that isn't going to change just because you develop a bit of a drug and hooker habit."

"I'm done with all of that shit, I swear on my life."

"Good." I smile and study him for a few seconds, trying to pinpoint where this change is coming from. The guy Archer hired must be some sort of miracle worker to have turned Jude around so quickly. "May I ask what brought on the change? Was the dude Archer hired *that* good at his job?"

Jude blushes and squirms a little before squaring his shoulders and meeting my eyes.

"I'm seeing Archer and Bennett. It's not a typical relationship, I guess?"

"What do you mean?"

"Bennett, the guy Archer hired, is my... um...my Dom," he explains, squirming a bit again, but holding my gaze like he's determined not to look ashamed. "And Archer is my Daddy."

Well, *that* was not what I was expecting. My mind whirls for a few seconds, searching for the right response.

"I went to a kink club once and let a Dom work me over on the St. Andrews Cross. I don't think it was my thing, but hey, whatever floats your boat."

"I don't know what that is," Jude laughs. "It's mostly like spanking and stuff."

"It's clearly working for you, so I'm happy to hear it."

"Thanks. I guess I should get out of your hair and let you get back to whoever you have tied up back there."

"Making him wait is half the fun," I continue to lie, feeling bad now that Jude just admitted something that was clearly difficult for him, but it feels like it would be way too weird to admit the truth now. "Thank you for coming over and for telling me about Archer and Bennett."

Jude stands up, and I start to lead him to the door, before he stops and looks at me again, his eyes full of vulnerability. "Do you think there's any chance if we sign a new contract with Epic that they'll let us lighten our schedule a bit?"

"I'm not sure. But I can't imagine Lincoln or Lando will be all that open to keeping the schedule we had before. And, in all honesty, things have changed for me too, I think." Maybe if the band *does* stay together, and our schedule gets less crazy, Paris and I can see what this thing between us really is.

"So, if they won't agree to give us some breathing room, we're going to walk?"

"I think so. But let's wait and talk about it when Lincoln is back in the city next month, okay?" I don't want to think about the possibility of things not working out. I've thought about it way too much in the past month, and it feels like I have more to lose than ever before if everything falls apart.

"Yeah," Jude says.

"Stay out of trouble," I say with a wink, opening the door for Jude and waving as he steps onto the elevator to leave.

As I head back into my bedroom and slip between the sheets with Paris, I can't help but feel hopeful about the future of the band. If Jude can get his shit together, surely there's hope. Right?

TRACK 29: SIDE A

Fresh Start

Benji

My stomach is fluttering with nerves as I ride the elevator up to the third floor of Epic Records. This is it, after everything we've been through, it all comes down to this band meeting.

After Jude came to visit me a couple of weeks ago, I've allowed myself to hope that maybe things could turn around for Downward Spiral, but that hope has come with a heavy dose of skepticism. I've been afraid to get too excited at the thought, afraid if I do, it'll inevitably go to shit. So, I'm going into this meeting with no expectations whatsoever.

My phone vibrates in my pocket, and I pull it out to see a text from Paris.

Paris: No matter what happens today, it's all going to be fine

Benji: Thank you. I needed to hear that

Paris: Any time. Call me later to tell me how it goes.

Benji: Will do

Paris has heard every hope and doubt I've had over the past few weeks as I've swung from one mood to the next. I'm surprised he hasn't had me committed.

Stepping off the elevator, I head down the hall to the room the label allowed us to use for our meeting today. I take a deep breath and say a little prayer before turning the handle on the conference room door and stepping inside.

"Hey man, come on in. We're just talking about what assholes we all were and promising we'll be together forever and all that sappy shit," Jude says, waving me in. A rush of relief hits me in the chest as I take in the three of them sitting around the conference table, smiling and all looking healthier than I've seen them in years.

"It's about time you all pulled your heads out of your asses," I joke, going around the table to sit next to Lincoln.

"We'll have to all make sure to thank Archer for forcing us to take a vacation; it seems to have done the trick," Lincoln says.

"Oh, I think Jude has the thanking covered for all of us," I tease, and Jude blushes. *Jude*, the dude who's literally done coke off a prostitute's ass right in front of me, fucking blushes.

"Dude," Jude complains, and Lando lights up with excitement.

"I fucking knew it," he crows.

"Wait, knew what?" Lincoln asks.

"I'm seeing Archer," Jude admits. "And Bennett, the guy Archer hired to help me get back on track," Jude explains, and I give him an encouraging nod to let him know I have his back. Lando and Lincoln take it in stride, asking a few questions about how it works and then telling him to keep it up if it's making him this happy.

"Okay, we can get back to gossiping about our boyfriends in a little bit, but first, I think we should get down to what this meeting is really about," Lincoln suggests. "The schedule we've been maintaining for the past ten years has been killing us. I think we need to tell the label that we'll only re-sign if we can tour less and have shorter tours when we do. And, we need time off in between recording new albums."

We all nod in agreement. It's obvious we're all on the same page, and I have a feeling their new relationship statuses have a lot to do with it. I listen to them swap information about their new boyfriends while I bask in the glow of Downward Spiral rising from the flames. I was sure were about to be devoured by those flames. The band isn't breaking up. I want to call Paris and tell him the good news, but first I think a little bit of bonding time for the four of us is in order.

"Great, let's go hit the bar across the street and gossip about our boyfriends then," I suggest, and they all happily agree.

Jude calls Bennett, and then we all head

across the street to a little pub.

I can't remember the last time the four of us just *hung out*. Sure, we've been crammed onto tour busses together nearly constantly, but even in that confined space, we seemed to find ways to avoid each other. I didn't realize until this moment just how far we'd grown apart. But, as we all sit around the round bar table in the dim light of the place, all smiling and relaxed for the first time in years, this feels like a brand new chapter for us.

"I want you guys to know my coke habit is under control now," Jude says after a waitress comes over to take our orders. "I know I'm never *not* going to be an addict, but I'm going to work really fucking hard not to derail my life again like I did."

I reach over and clap Jude on the shoulder to show my support, and then Lincoln and Lando each do the same.

A few weeks ago, Lincoln did a TV interview to talk about recently being diagnosed with bipolar disorder, so he tells us about his new medication and the therapist he's been seeing. I make a mental note to do research when I get home on supporting recovering addicts as well as learning as much as I can about Lincoln's diagnosis. Somewhere along the way, I forgot these men are my brothers, but I'm not going to do that again. I'm not naive; now that they're both on the right track that doesn't mean it's going to be smooth sailing from here on out. But this time I'm going to make sure I know how to support them the right way to help them back up when they fall.

"I'm really proud of both of you," Lando says, and I nod in agreement.

"I know we've been dead weight for years, but I want you guys to know I appreciate the way you held the band together and kept Jude and me propped up the best you could," Lincoln says to Lando and me.

"Oh man, this is getting sappy. Benji, tell us about the hot sex with your new boyfriend," Jude says, changing the subject as we all laugh.

"Yeah, what's up with that? You dated London, and now you're getting it on with his twin brother?" Lincoln asks.

"Ugh," I groan. "I never dated London, for the love of all that's holy."

"Still, all of a sudden you're with his brother?" Lando adds, cocking his head with curiosity.

"Truth be told..." I'm about to admit that we're not *really* dating, it's just for publicity, but somehow a deeper truth pops out of my mouth. "I always had a thing for Paris; I just didn't think it was mutual."

"How does London feel about it?" Lincoln asks.

"Oh god, he's more excited than Paris and I are."

"Good, it's good to see you happy," Lando says.

"I've always been happy," I point out.

"I thought so too, but there's something different now. Like, it was surface happy before, and now, it's the real thing," Jude muses, studying me with a too-perceptive gaze.

"Okay, the interrogation of Benji is over, who's next?" I joke, holding my hands up in surrender. All the guys laugh, and we move on to grilling Lando about Dawson. This is how the band was supposed to be all along, close, happy, family.

*****

Less than an hour after we all part ways at the bar after our little celebration, a group text sent from Jude pings my phone.

Jude: The label fired Archer
Lincoln: What?????
Lando: No fucking way
Benji: How can they do that?
Jude: I'm sorry, guys, but I'm *not* re-signing with them now
Lincoln: Agreed. Can we all get together and talk about this?
Jude: I'm at Bennett's

Jude's text is followed by an address, and we all say we'll be there ASAP.

Lincoln, Lando, and I meet in the lobby of Bennett's building and ride up on the elevator together, all fuming at the new development.

"How can they do this to him?" Lando rants. "He discovered us; he's been with us from the beginning. I can't imagine Downward Spiral with a different manager."

"We're not going to have a different manager," I agree firmly.

We get off on Bennett's floor, and Jude greets us at the door. As soon as we're inside, we waste no time expressing our outrage over the situation, shouting and vowing justice on Archer's behalf.

"Quiet," Bennett commands loudly, and we all fall silent in an instant. "One at a time please, and let's keep this productive rather than just bitching about something we can't change."

"Wow, he's really good at that," I stage whisper to Jude who nods knowingly.

"Tell me about it," he agrees before turning to all of us and saying more or less the same thing he said in his text. "If they don't want Archer, they're not getting me."

A murmur of agreement goes around the room, all of us completely on the same page about not re-signing with Epic if this is the way they're going to treat Archer.

"Guys, think this through. If you walk and go to another label, there's no guarantee I'll be able to follow you there. It doesn't make sense for you to leave Epic just because of me," Archer reasons.

Jude gets up from his spot and goes to kneel in front of Archer. I've never seen Jude look so sweet or reverent before. If there was ever any doubt that what Jude has with Archer and Bennett is real, it was dispelled in that instant.

"Daddy," he says quietly. "We wouldn't be anything without you. If nothing else, I don't want Epic to make another dime off us."

"Hey, Archer," Lando pipes in. "Haven't you always wanted your own label?"

Archer tears his gaze from Jude and looks over his head at Lando, eyes wide.

"I can't start my own label just like *that*." He snaps his fingers. "It costs a lot of money."

"Um, Archie, you *have* a lot of money," Bennett points out helpfully.

"But..." Archer shakes his head, trying to pull up a new argument.

"What if we invest in it? Is that a thing?" Lincoln asks. "The four of us, plus you, it'll be no problem."

The thought sends a jolt of excitement through me. If we're part owners of the label, not only would we have our own music, we'd be able to help other artists too. We can help bring on new bands and give them to the world.

"What better position could you possibly want for starting your own label? You'll have the highest grossing rock band on the planet signed to you. And...I might know a few other bands who would be interested," I reason.

"This is crazy," Archer protests.

"It's not crazy," Bennett argues. "It's what you've been working toward."

"I can't take you guys' money."

"It's an investment, and you're hardly going to bankrupt us," Jude points out. "Say yes, Daddy."

Archer looks around the room at us, and then at Bennett, who gives him a smile and a small shrug to say *What do you have to lose?*

"Honestly, Archer, I *want* to do this. I think it would be amazing. We're not going to be rock stars forever, and it would be amazing to be part owner in a label like this."

He bites his lip and looks back at Jude one last time, and then his face splits into a smile of his own. "Okay, yes."

The guys whoop, and Jude scrambles onto Archer's lap, covering his face in kisses until we all groan in protest at the display.

Paris

It's nearly midnight, and I'm just getting into bed when my phone starts to ring with a video call. I smile widely before even picking it up, knowing it'll be Benji.

"Hey, I thought you'd call me *hours* ago. How'd the meeting go?" I ask as soon as his face fills the screen. His hair is spread out around him on his pillow, and all the lights seem to be out. There's a smile on his lips, which I want to kiss so badly I can hardly breathe.

He tells me about the meeting and what happened with Archer.

"So, you're going to be part owner in a new record label?"

"It looks like it. We need to hammer out the details, and I get the feeling the other guys are down to invest but don't want to deal with much else, but I'm thinking of telling Archer I want to be a full partner."

"That's amazing."

"It's going to be a lot of work," he hedges, biting down on his bottom lip.

It takes me a second to get what he's saying. Last time I was in New York, there were some allusions to our relationship changing, but now Benji's taking on a whole new set of responsibilities.

"I understand. I'm still working things out too. I've been talking to my agent about motivational speaking, and I'm still considering some other things too. It's stressful, but it's exciting too."

"Yeah," he agrees, the worry lines between his eyebrows easing as he smiles again, playfully this time.

"You know a great way to ease stress?"

"Yeah, but it's a little late to go to the gym," I joke.

"Huh, guess we'll have to find another way to get our blood pumping then."

The camera moves, and I'm treated to an enticing view of his tented bedsheets. He slides his hand under them, and I moan quietly, my own cock coming fully to life as Benji's sheet moves with his jerking hand.

"God, I wish you were here," he groans, the sheet finally slipping to give me a good view of his hard cock, his fist wrapped tightly around it, moving up and down rapidly.

"Me too," I agree, reaching into my own boxers and stroking myself.

His rising moans amp up my own arousal until my balls are aching and I'm thrusting into my grip, fucking my hand.

"Oh fuck," Benji gasps and thick ropes of cum spurt from his cock, coating his fingers and landing on his stomach and chest.

I follow right after him, groaning loudly as my orgasm overtakes me, my chest heaving and my body heating as I come so hard I end up with cum on my chin.

"God damn, that was good," I pant, reaching for my shirt on the floor by the bed and using it as a cum rag.

"Mmmhmm," he agrees, sounding sleepy now. "So, aside from still trying to figure out the job stuff, how's everything else going? How's the shoulder?"

"It's as good as can be expected," I answer, settling onto my side, holding my phone in front of me so I can see Benji's face as his eyes grow tired. "I've been trying to get London to come visit me in Chicago, but he's a hard sell."

"Oh, that sounds so fun. I should come visit and get Donnie to meet me in Chicago too. We can all spend a weekend hanging out."

"That would be fun, but maybe wait a few more weeks; we have a bunch of snowstorms coming."

Benji sighs. "Yeah, I probably need to wait anyway so I can talk to Archer about getting this label up and running."

"What should we do when you come to visit?" I ask, my eyes starting to drift closed. He makes a number of suggestions ranging from deliciously filthy to outrageous, and I let his voice carry me off to sleep.

TRACK 30: SIDE A

Time Marches On

Benji

I step out of the car outside of Archer's gorgeous house in upstate California and quickly pull out my phone to snap a selfie with the house in the background. I send the message to Paris with a message about how much nicer the weather is than New York. We haven't seen each other since the end of January, almost six weeks ago now, and I swear I'm having withdrawals.

We've been texting and video calling almost every day, but with helping Archer get the new record label going, there hasn't been time for a visit. And Paris is just as busy. He's gone to give speeches at a couple of high schools in Chicago already and is talking about setting up more around the country. On top of that, he's been in talks with some sports network about possibly auditioning to be a full-time sportscaster.

Paris: Looks nice. Any chance there's a layover in Chicago on your way home?

Benji: I'll see what I can do

I pocket my phone and climb the steps to the front porch. Archer invited me out for the weekend to show me the recording studio in his basement and talk about plans for Archery Records. He's been hard at work getting the legal aspects set up, now the question is how aggressively we want to seek out artists, among other things.

Archer answers the door when I knock and ushers me inside with a huge smile in place. I don't know if it's the new record company, his new relationship with Jude and Bennett, or the fact that Lincoln and Jude are no longer keeping him awake at night with worry, but I've never seen him this happy. I swear he looks ten years younger.

"Hey, Arch, how's it going?" I ask as I step inside.

"I certainly can't complain."

"Awesome, did you get the logo mock-ups I emailed you?"

"I got the email but haven't looked at it. I'll do it now."

I wasn't sure how Archer was going to feel when I first went to him and told him I wanted to be more than just an investor—I wanted to be a partner in the company—but he seemed thrilled. The rest of the guys were happy to write checks and step back, but I see a future here long after Downward Spiral. The past six weeks getting things set up have been hectic but amazing.

He leads me into the kitchen where his laptop is sitting open at the table. My eyes land on a calendar stuck to the refrigerator that has star stickers on some of the days from this month.

"What's that about?"

Archer follows my gaze and blushes before drawing himself up confidently, reminding me of the night Jude told me about their *unconventional* relationship.

"It's a reward system for Jude," he explains. "Ben is great with discipline, but I think there's something to be said for positive reinforcement too."

"That makes sense," I nod, not entirely sure I can relate to their dynamic, but I'm certainly not about to judge what's clearly working so well for them. "You guys seem to be really happy, so whatever it is, keep doing what you're doing."

Archer blushes again and nods. "It's been a learning curve," he admits. "This may be something Ben knows backward and forward, but Jude and I are still figuring out how this works for us."

"That makes sense. Jude seems to be doing well though."

As soon as I say it, Jude walks into the kitchen. "Daddy," he says smiling, but as soon as his eyes dart to me, he tenses up a little. "Oh, I didn't realize Benji was here."

"It's okay, come here." Archer pats his lap, and Jude dips his head, avoiding my gaze as he climbs onto Archer's lap.

"What can I do for you?"

"I wanted to tell you I finished my chores for the day."

"Good job; go get a sticker." Archer kisses Jude's forehead, and I can't help but be stunned at the sweetness of the interaction. Jude gets back off his lap and goes to the drawer beside the fridge, pulls out a sticker, and puts it on the calendar.

"Benji and I are having a business meeting and then maybe we can all go out for dinner."

"Okay, Daddy."

I'm still in shock as Jude leaves the kitchen. It's completely at odds with the Jude I've always known, but in the best possible way.

"I guess that answers that question," I say with a laugh.

"He's doing well," Archer agrees. "He still has his struggles. He's only a few months sober, so it's not like it's all sunshine and rainbows, but I think the structure Bennett's giving him is really helping him."

"I have a feeling the love and support he's getting from you is making a big impact too."

"I hope so."

A quiet love radiates from Archer as a smile tilts his lips. Eventually he gets focused again and pulls up the logo mock-ups for us to take a look at.

After that, he shows me the recording studio in his basement where Downward Spiral, as well as Last Weekend, and any other bands we sign in the near future, will be recording their albums.

"Just think, we might create music history right here," I muse, taking a seat in the swivel chair in front of the mixing board.

"Here's hoping," Archer agrees with a smile.

Paris

As soon as I step inside my apartment, I kick off my shoes and toss my keys on the little table by the door. It reminds me of the fancy table at Benji's place, and I instantly wish I could get on a plane to New York. Except, he's not in New York; he's in California trying to get a new business off the ground. He's in over his head launching the next step of his career, just like I am. But that doesn't stop me from missing the hell out of him.

The media have lost interest in our relationship over the past few weeks, but we've amassed quite a following on Instagram and Twitter of people enthralled by our supposed love story. Thank god, the hashtag they came up with isn't some cutesy mashup of our names; it's just #BenjiandParis. I can live with that, although I *do* wonder why he has first billing.

Our fake relationship has outlived its initial purpose, but neither of us has mentioned ending it. It doesn't feel like an act—it never really did, and if we aren't in a place to make things *real*, I want to keep faking it as long as possible.

I flop down on my couch and pull out my phone to call London.

"Hey, what's up?" he says when he answers.

"Not much, just got home after giving a speech at another high school in the city. I got an email from my agent about guest hosting on *Sports Night* for a week as sort of an audition."

"That's fantastic."

"Is it?" I ask, cringing a little at how ungrateful I probably seem. "I mean, yeah the paycheck would be incredible if I landed it, but it feels so...pointless."

"You can do a lot of good with a stupidly large paycheck," he points out.

"True." And I don't want to mention it, but the show *does* film in New York, which is a huge point in its favor. But Benji might not even be staying in New York. With the rest of the band on the west coast now, I wouldn't be surprised if he decided to move too. And how pathetic would that be if I took a job I barely even wanted just to move near a guy I'm not even really dating.

"At least do the trial week. You never know, you might like it."

"Yeah, maybe," I agree halfheartedly. "Hey, you should come see me. Benji might stop through Chicago this weekend; we could all hang out."

"I can probably swing that."

"Awesome, I'll get you a plane ticket." I sit up and reach for my laptop.

"You don't have to do that."

"It's no big deal. I can afford it. Plus, you shouldn't have to drive eight hours both ways just to hang out for the weekend, that's stupid."

"Fine, I won't argue with you on that one."

I book him a flight for tomorrow night, and we chat a little while longer before hanging up. Once we do, I put in a call to my agent to tell her I'll do the trial week for *Sports Night*. Worst case scenario, I'll hate it, but I'll get to spend a week in New York with Benji. It could be worse.

*****

Standing in airport pickup, I glance down at the hibiscus flower in my hand and wonder if it's overkill. It seemed like a sweet idea when I put in a special order for it, but now I feel like it might be a little much.

Before I can spend too much time over-thinking it, I spot Benji coming through the crowd with his suitcase in tow and his long, blond hair billowing around him like he's on the runway. When he sees me, his face lights up. My chest warms, and I cease to care whether the flower is tipping my hand. He pushes past people, not bothering to apologize, his attention fixed on me alone, my heart racing.

He breaks out into nearly a run as he gets closer, and for a second I'm worried he's going to try to jump into my arms. I'm out of my sling, but nowhere near strong enough to hold him up if he tries it. Luckily, he just slams into me, carefully directing the majority of his body weight against my left side as I wrap my arms around him, careful not to crush the flower.

"I missed you," he murmurs against my neck as he buries his face there, followed by a kiss against my Adam's apple.

"Missed you, too," I say against his hair, kissing the top of his head.

"How's the shoulder?"

"Getting better. I'm on top of my PT, and it's getting stronger. It'll never be one hundred percent again, but after having it in a sling for over a month, I'm just glad to be able to use it again." I pull back and hold the flower out to him a little shyly.

"For me?" he asks with a pleased smile.

"It's kind of sappy…"

"I love it." Benji takes the flower and tilts his head up for a kiss. "When does London's flight get in?"

"Another half hour."

We decide to take a seat while we wait, and Benji fills me in on everything going on with Archery Records, and I tell him about *Sports Night*. It's on the tip of my tongue more than once to say something about our arrangement, to tell him I want to be more, that I think I might be falling in love with him. But I'm too afraid that he'll tell me it's still not a good time, so I keep my mouth shut.

London arrives right on time, and we both greet him with a hug. When I was in the NFL, I went most of the year without seeing my brother typically, but for some reason, the past two months seems so much longer. I've missed him.

"How's it been going, bro?"

"I can't complain."

"Sure, you can. I've heard you complain *many* times," Benji teases, and London gives him the finger.

"Let's go drop your stuff off at my place and then we can decide what we want to do this weekend," I suggest.

We order an Uber and all cram into the back seat, Benji between London and me. He leans into my side, and I put my arm around him so he can put his head on my shoulder.

London eyes us and then gives me a look, raising his eyebrows at me and clearly calling me out without words. I know he thought we were full of shit when we said this was casual, and it's clear he hasn't changed his opinion.

When we get up to my apartment, London drops his bag by the couch, and I tell Benji he can put his in my bedroom.

"Want to show me where?" Benji asks suggestively, waggling his eyebrows at me.

London sighs and grabs the TV remote, clicking it on and cranking up the volume. I give him an appreciative smile and follow Benji into the bedroom, closing the door behind us.

Benji drops his suitcase carelessly and spins toward me, pulling me in for a proper kiss now that we're alone. His lips are hot and needy against mine, and I tangle one hand in his hair and use the other to grip his waist, pulling his body against mine.

"God, two months is too long," he complains against my mouth, pulling away and wiggling out of his pants. He drops them to the floor, and then his eyes seem to catch on something because he freezes, his hands on the hem of his shirt.

"You okay?" I ask.

"Hm?" He turns his head back in my direction. "Oh yeah, I'm good," he says, forcing a smile. When he looks away again, I follow his gaze and see a box of condoms on the floor by my bed. Is that what upset him? Does he think I've been with anyone else since I saw him last? Has *he*? I wouldn't blame him if he had; two months is a long time to go when you have people throwing themselves at you, dying for a chance to say they were fucked by someone famous. But the thought of him with anyone else twists my stomach and makes me feel sick.

"There hasn't been anyone else, if that's what you're wondering," I tell him. "I tossed them by the bed when I was unpacking and never thought about it again."

Visible relief washes over him. "It's none of my business," he says, clearly trying to play it cool

"Casual or not, Benji, we're sleeping together, which makes it your business," I tell him firmly. "Have you...I mean, has there been—"

He cuts me off with another kiss, pressing his half-naked body against mine, his cock dragging against the rough denim of the jeans I still have on, our skin seeming to heat on contact. His lips part, and I thrust my tongue inside, moaning at the taste of him. I run my fingers through his silky hair, tugging it as he kisses me deeper, holds me tighter.

"There's no one else," he answers when we part, both gasping for breath.

The relief is so strong it nearly buckles my knees. And a little flare of hope lights in my chest that he might feel the same way I do.

TRACK 31: SIDE A

Maybe

Paris

When I climb into an Uber outside of JFK airport, the weather is a complete one-eighty from the last time I was in New York in January. The sun is shining, all the snow is gone, and it has to be near seventy degrees.

My week-long trial for *Sports Night* got pushed back more than once to the point I was about to say *fuck it, never mind*, when they *finally* made it happen this week. I start tomorrow and film through Friday, and then I'll hear back after that if they're interested in offering me a full-time position sitting at a desk talking sports news with a few other people for a stupid amount of money. I'm still not convinced it's what I want to do, but I figure an audition can't hurt.

As soon as I hop in the back of the Uber, I pull out my phone to call Benji.

"Hey, aren't you supposed to be on an airplane right now?"

"I caught an earlier flight; I'm already in

265

the city," I tell him.

"Dammit, why do you keep doing this to me?" he complains. "Can you wait at the airport so I can come pick you up?"

"I'm already in an Uber."

"It's not fair you're allowed to come pick me up at the airport with flowers and shit, but you *never* tell me when your flights are getting in."

"I'm sorry," I say with a chuckle. "I'll be at your place shortly, and I'll see if I can make it up to you."

"Oh, wait, I'm not at home. I didn't expect you for hours still, so I'm at Nathan's Pub on the corner of my block getting a drink with the guys."

"Want me to meet you there or hang outside your building for a bit?"

"Come here. You haven't seen the guys in ages; they'll be excited to see you."

"Okay, I'll see you soon."

We hang up, and I give the driver the new drop off location.

The bar is busy, even for the middle of the day on a Saturday, but it's not difficult to spot the crowded table of rock stars in the corner. Benji has a huge smile on his face as he says something to his bandmates, gesturing wildly as they all laugh. For a second it feels like I'm transported back in time, covertly watching Benji and his friends during lunch period. I wanted to go over and sit with them so badly, find a way to soak up Benji and just be in his presence. I would've given anything to be part of his world the way London was. Maybe it was strange, because to the outside world he was some effeminate band nerd while I was the popular quarterback, but I laid awake at night wishing I could trade places with my brother. God, I had it bad for Benji. *I guess not much has changed.* I laugh and shake my head at myself.

Benji's eye catches mine, and he waves me over to the table.

"Well, if it isn't Mr. Star Quarterback," Lincoln greets me teasingly.

"Not anymore," I chuckle.

"Oh shit, yeah, sorry that was a total dick thing to say." He cringes and apologizes.

"No worries, I'm slowly getting over it."

"If you keep half as busy as Benji does, I'm sure you have plenty to distract yourself."

"I don't know if anyone keeps as busy as Benji," I say.

"Says the man who's been trying out different careers left and right," Benji teases.

"Fine, we're both busy," I agree, meeting his gaze and smiling as warmth spreads through my body, and the pit of my stomach flutters. Would it be rude to haul Benji out of here and drag him back to his place so I can get him naked? It's been two months since he stopped in Chicago for the weekend on his way home from

California, and four months since we've had more than forty-eight hours together. I wonder if he's missed me half as much as I've missed him.

As if he can read the question in my eyes, a soft smile paints his lips, and he gives me the barest of nods.

"If you guys are going to sit here eye fucking each other, you might as well just go home," Jude complains.

"Oh please, like you can talk," Benji counters, rolling his eyes at the drummer. He pats the open seat beside himself, and I round the table, setting my suitcase down on the floor and hanging my suit bag over the back of the chair. Then, I turn to Benji and wrap my arms around him, hauling him out of his chair to kiss the hell out of him.

My shoulder twinges, but I ignore it, far more concerned with my lips on his than anything else in the world. He wraps his arms around my neck, and I sweep my tongue into his mouth, savoring his sweet flavor and drinking down the little sounds he makes.

It's on the tip of my tongue to tell him how much I've missed him, to say *fuck casual*, to beg him to tell me this has become as real for him as it is for me. But I don't say any of it, instead I pour my heart into the kiss and hope like hell he feels some fraction of what I'm feeling for him.

"I'm glad you're here," Benji says when we finally break the kiss.

"Me too."

"You want a drink?" Lando asks, waving down the waitress, as I settle into my chair.

I order a beer, and everyone else orders a second round, except for Jude who gets a soda.

"So, what are you all doing in New York? I thought Benji was the only one still living here."

"I still live here for now, too," Lando says.

"I'm here gathering up the shit I actually want from my penthouse so I can get it sold and be done with it," Lincoln explains.

"And Bennett had some work to do in New York this month, I figured with Da—" Jude stops himself and blushes. "With Archer so busy back in California, I might as well tag along out here."

"Dude, don't censor yourself. No one here cares that you call Archer Daddy," Benji says, and Jude blushes an even darker shade of red before nodding.

"Thank you. I guess I'm still getting used to it."

"Let your freak flag fly, my friend," Benji advises, holding up his glass for a toast.

"To freak flags," I supply, and everyone repeats it with a laugh, clanging our glasses together.

Benji

We hang out at the bar with the guys for another hour before I can't wait any longer to get Paris back to my place so I can have my way with him.

"All right, we're heading out," I declare, standing up and throwing a wad of bills on the table to cover our drinks and a more than generous tip.

"Have fun," Lando says suggestively.

"And take the week off while your man is here. God knows you've been doing *more* than your fair share for the label; you can afford a little down time."

I'm sure the guilt is showing on my face. Maybe I've been overdoing it a *little* bit, but I love the work I've been doing for the label—getting in contact with graphic artists we can contract for album covers, meeting with PR firms and marketing agencies to decide who we want to work with, the list goes on and on. "I like doing the work for Archery Records."

"I know, and it's awesome, but you're going to burn yourself out if you don't focus on yourself and your life outside of working too."

"Thank you for your input. Now, if you don't mind, I'm going to take Paris home so we can be naked."

The guys catcall at us as I grab Paris' hand and drag him out of the bar.

On the way back to my place, he fills me in on this job he's auditioning for this week. If he gets offered a full-time position, it would mean moving to New York permanently. Two months ago I would've been over the moon at the thought, but with the new recording studio on the West Coast, and Lincoln and Jude living out there, I'm sure Lando will follow soon. How long will it make sense for *me* to stay in New York? Paris might move out here just for me to have to up and move to the opposite side of the country.

That thought makes my chest feel hollow, and I reach up to rub it. I know we both have busy lives, probably too busy for a relationship, but every time we're together, it feels less and less casual. For me, anyway. For all I know, Paris is more than happy with the current arrangement.

I greet my doorman with a friendly wave and then key in the elevator code to my floor. As soon as the elevator doors close, I push Paris up against the mirrored wall and devour his lips. I slip my hands under his shirt and slide them along his muscled abs. He hasn't let his workouts slip since his injury, that's for sure. I can feel his cock hardening against me through our layers of clothes and mine does the same as I grind against him, licking and nipping at his lips.

The elevator dings open on my floor just in time, because if it hadn't, my doorman would be getting quite the show from the camera on the elevator.

"I need you inside me so badly."

"Then you'd better get us inside your place, or I'm going to lose my patience and take you right here in the hallway," he warns in a husky voice.

"Is that supposed to be a threat, because anything that gets you inside me faster is fine with me."

Paris groans and plucks my key out of my hand, shoving it into the lock and pushing my door open so fast it bangs against the wall. We stumble inside in a blur of hands and mouths, our clothes being shed haphazardly. I don't know where he puts the key, and I couldn't give less of a shit about it.

We end up naked on the floor less than two feet from the door, Paris' body pinning me down as I moan against his skin, kissing his chest and throat. His cock is velvet steel against mine, my legs wrapped around his waist as he humps against me.

"Missed you so much," he murmurs against my ear, nuzzling and then flicking his tongue against it. "Missed your lips and your body. Missed your smile and your body in bed next to me when I wake up in the morning."

My heart goes wild at his words, my entire body feeling like it's on fire as I buck up to meet his thrusts.

"God, I missed you too, 'Ris," I moan, digging my fingers into the firm muscles of his ass cheeks, encouraging him to move faster. Pre-cum leaks from my slit, and my balls grow heavy and tight as heat starts to pool in my stomach. Some part of my brain protests against finishing this way, desperate to feel Paris filling and stretching me. But the more desperate part of me reasons that condoms and lube are *way* too far away right now, and we have plenty of time to fuck all week.

"So good, Benji. So fucking hot and perfect. I can't get enough of you," Paris groans, fucking against me faster, his chest heaving against mine as our cries grow louder, both of our bodies slick with sweat, muscles taut as we chase our orgasms.

"Oh fuck, oh fuck," I pant, biting down on his collarbone as pleasure washes over me, my cock throbbing against his as I cover us both in hot, sticky seed. Paris humps faster, his whole body trembling before he lets out a strangled cry, and his release joins mine in coating us.

"Hey, 'Ris?"

"Yeah?" he answers, still breathing heavily.

"Why'd you avoid me all those years? Were you pissed about that kiss?"

"Kiss?"

"Yeah, when I was drunk and kissed you at our graduation party." The band left on our first tour a week later, and Paris went away to college shortly after; it was the last time I saw him for ten years, and I always wondered what he thought of that kiss. Liquid courage was the only reason I was able to go through with it, and I could've sworn he was into it too, and recent evidence suggests he's attracted to me, but it hasn't stopped me from wondering about it.

"You knew it was me?"

I turn my head and look at Paris with an expression on my face that hopefully conveys how crazy he sounds right now.

"Duh. Who else would it have been?"

"I always assumed you thought I was London," he explains.

And then everything clicks into place. "You thought I kissed you by mistake, and you felt bad because you liked it so much?"

"Maybe," he mutters in response, an embarrassed expression creeping over his face.

"I've been able to tell you and London apart since right after I met you both. I knew it was you."

The smile that breaks out over his face nearly takes my breath away. It's so beautiful I can't help but kiss him, just so I can taste the happiness on his lips.

We lay on the floor with sweat and cum cooling on our skin, kissing and talking, for some time until I finally push him off of me, and we clean ourselves up before climbing into bed to lay together a little while longer.

"Hey, Benji? This doesn't feel so casual anymore, does it?" Paris asks, anxiety clear in his voice. With my cheek resting on his chest, I can feel his heart beating faster.

"No, it doesn't," I agree. Tilting my head so

I'm looking at him, I ask, "What should we do about that?"

"Well, we both agreed we had too much on our plates right now for a relationship," he hedges.

"We did, but I've been finding it difficult to give a shit about anything on my plate aside from you," I admit.

His relief is visible as a smile spreads across his lips. "Me too."

His lips are on mine, his tongue sweeping into his mouth as we grab onto each other like desperate men lost at sea. He tunnels his fingers into my hair and holds me closer while we kiss.

"Does this mean we've upgraded from fake boyfriends to real ones?" I ask, smiling against his lips.

"Fuck yes."

TRACK 32: SIDE A

Walk in The Park

Paris

I think I'm more nervous stepping into the *Sports Night* studio on Monday morning than I was stepping onto the field in an NFL jersey for the first time. Benji woke up early and took a shower with me, saying that a shower blowjob is the only acceptable way to start the day. I'm not going to lie: he was damn convincing. Then, he laid naked in bed, watching me get dressed. And if that wasn't the most distracting thing ever, I don't know what is.

He sent me off with a kiss and the promise of a *proper* first date tonight. So, even if this day sucks, or I make an ass of myself on national TV, at least I have that to look forward to.

People bustle around the set as I try to figure out where exactly I'm supposed to go. My palms sweat, and my heart beats fast. I swear, I'd rather have a four-hundred-pound lineman bearing down on me right now.

"Paris," someone calls my name, and I look around until I spot Van, one of the regular hosts of the show. He's a retired baseball player and has been a mainstay of the network for years. We've never met in person, but he waves me over happily.

I weave my way through all of the people and equipment until I reach him. He's standing in front of a large table, laid out with enough food—and fancy food at that—to feed an army.

"Hi, nice to meet you." I offer my hand, and he takes it.

"Good to meet you, too," he says. "I've been hoping for the chance for a few years, actually," he admits.

"You have?"

"Yeah. When I was playing pro-ball, I wished like hell I had the courage you did to come out. I know it was a different time when I played, and I probably would've lost my job, but staying in the closet cost me a lot more than my career."

"I'm sorry to hear that." I had *no* idea Van was gay, which I guess is his point.

"Me too," he says with a sigh. "But I think the work you're doing talking to high school athletes in Chicago is so important."

I can feel my face heating a little at the praise. How he found out about that work, I have no idea, but I'm glad to know other gay athletes agree there's a need for it.

"Thank you."

"You ready for this?" he asks, nodding toward the news desk we'll be sitting at with a few other people in a few minutes.

"Um…"

He chuckles and claps me on the back. "You'll be fine. I was so nervous I puked right before I filmed my first time and look where I am now."

I feel a little better knowing he's been where I am. "Okay, but if I say something stupid, kick me under the desk, okay?"

"You got it," he agrees.

The other sportscasters show up a few minutes later, and we spend a few minutes chatting before we get the signal that it's time to get ready on set.

"You've got this," Van assures me one more time as we take our seats. "And if you have to vomit, aim it away from me, please."

"I'll do my best," I laugh.

Benji

"How'd it go?" I ask as soon as Paris steps into the living room after taking off his shoes. He unbuttons the top button of his dress shirt and collapses next to me.

"I didn't make an ass of myself, so better than expected."

"Yay." I kiss him. "So, do you think you'll take the job full-time after this week?" I ask, trying to sound casual. I'm over the moon that we decided to make things official last night, but that doesn't erase the fact that we might still end up living three-thousand miles apart.

"First of all, I have to see if they even *offer* the job," he says.

"But if they do?"

"Well, you're here in New York..." He looks at me a little shyly, and I realize I've never mentioned that I'm probably going to need to relocate.

"For now, but with the rest of the band on the West Coast, and Archery Records out in California, moving may make the most sense for me."

"Oh, I didn't realize."

"Nothing's decided. Why don't we put a pin in this and just see what happens?" I suggest.

"That works," he agrees, giving me another kiss. "Now, I'm going to change, and then you promised me a date."

"I did," I agree with a smile.

While Paris gets changed, I call down to my driver to make sure we're ready to go. I already prepared earlier by loading the things I needed into the car. A sappy sort of excitement flutters in my stomach.

As soon as we get into the car, Paris starts asking where we're going for our date. I smile and kiss him to distract him from questions.

"Don't think I don't know what you're doing," he says against my lips.

"Kissing you?" I feign innocence.

"Distracting me."

"Hmm, is it working?"

"Yes," he says with a chuckle, and I kiss him deeper.

The car stops at Central Park, and we both climb out. Paris looks around curiously, no doubt wondering what kind of date we'll be having here, and then he sees the picnic basket and blanket I pull out of the trunk, and he smiles.

"We're having a picnic?"

"And a horse drawn carriage ride around the park," I say. "Is that way too cheesy for a first date?"

"It's perfect."

We walk hand and hand through the park looking for the best place to sit and enjoy our dinner. For a change, the absolute last thing on my mind is whether anyone is taking our picture or Tweeting about us. I'm more than happy just to *be* with Paris.

We pick a shady spot and spread out the blanket to sit down.

"To be honest, I thought you'd plan something a little fancier or more upscale. Like, taking me to the most highly rated and most expensive sushi place in the city or something," Paris admits as I open the basket and start to pull out the food I bought from the deli near my place.

I freeze with a sandwich held halfway out to Paris.

"I'm sorry; did I fuck this up? We can ditch

the picnic, and I can take you somewhere impressive."

"No, god no," Paris hurries to reassure me. "I love this. It's so much better than somewhere expensive and fancy. This is...*romantic*." He blushes a little as he says the last word, and I make a mental note that Paris loves romance and vow to spend the rest of my life being the most romantic fool he's ever met.

"So, aside from working my ass off on Archery Records, there's something else I've been doing a lot of research on lately," I tell him as we dig into our food.

"Oh yeah? What is it?"

"I set up an appointment with some people to find out how to go about starting an LGBTQ teen foundation," I explain. "You told me before it might be a big job for just one person."

It seems to take a second for him to process what I'm saying, but as soon as he does, his eyes light up, his whole face lights up.

"I'm in. Tell me when and where the meeting is and I'm there."

I smile and lean forward to kiss him.

"It's in a few weeks. I'll give you all the info when we get back home after our date."

"Sounds good. What do you have in mind for it?"

"I'm picturing sort of an after-school center where LGBT kids can get together and hang out, just be themselves. I'd love to offer music therapy and maybe some other things eventually. I guess the idea isn't fully formed yet, but it's a starting point?"

"Absolutely. We can brainstorm some more ideas," Paris says. "I do have an idea for a name."

"Yeah, tell me. I've been stuck on names."

"OUTshine."

"I love that. OUTshine it is."

"Wow, we go from fake boyfriends to real boyfriends and business partners in the span of twenty-four hours," he says with a laugh.

"Full speed ahead, baby," I joke, giving him a playful wink. "'Ris, I want you to know, I'm *all* in on this," I tell him more seriously, reaching over to put my hand on his.

"Me too. Full speed ahead," he repeats, picking up my hand and giving me a kiss on the back of it.

After we finish eating, we pack up our picnic and go to where the horse drawn carriage rides board. Paris climbs in first and turns around to offer me his hand to help me up. We settle in, and he puts his arm around my shoulders, and I spread the blanket out over our laps, since it's getting a little chilly now that the sun is starting to set.

The carriage lurches forward, and I laugh as we both jolt in our seats. Leaning my head against Paris' shoulder, we fall into a peaceful silence. The *clip clop* of the horse's hooves is the perfect drumline for the normal music of the city. I tap my foot to the beat as it plays all around us.

"Listening to that music in your head?" Paris teases.

"It's not in my head, silly. It's all around us; you just need to know how to listen."

TRACK 33: SIDE A

Chicago

Benji

Maybe I should've called to tell Paris I'd be in Chicago this weekend, but a surprise seemed like more fun. It seemed like more fun before I found myself standing in the hallway of his apartment building, wondering if he's home. For all I know he's in LA or god knows where else. I would've liked to think he would've told me that, but we're still figuring out this whole *boyfriend* thing.

I finally hear footsteps on the other side of the door, followed by the click of the lock, and the door swings open. Paris is wearing a team jersey and a pair of jeans that hug his thighs enticingly.

"Holy shit," he says, his face breaking into a huge smile as he steps forward and pulls me into his arms. "What are you doing here?"

"There's this local band whose demo Archer got ahold of, and he was planning to come out and check them out in person. But I volunteered to do it instead since he has so much going on getting the label up and running."

"So, you didn't come to see me?" he asks, arching an eyebrow at me before he steers me inside his apartment.

"Nah," I tease, turning back to him and pressing a brief kiss to his lips. "You up for going with me to check out the band tonight?"

"Yeah. How soon do we have to leave?" he asks, nuzzling my throat, his hands roaming over my ass and giving it a squeeze.

"In about two orgasms."

He barks out a laugh, a puff of warm breath hitting my skin. I can feel the smile on his lips, still pressed to my Adam's apple. "I *love* that measure of time."

He doesn't stop kissing me as he walks me backward down the hall until we reach his bedroom. When he finally releases me, I grab the hem of my shirt and pull it over my head while he does the same.

"Will you fuck me?" he asks.

My eyes go wide, and my mouth drops open. "I didn't think you were vers."

"I had a bad experience once, and since then, I only bottom after I've been with someone a while, once I know I can trust them," he explains, a hint of vulnerability filling his expression and hitting me right in the chest. This is no off handed request; he's giving me something he doesn't give to just anyone.

"I'd love to." I kiss him one more time,

slow and sweet.

As our lips find a rhythm, I run my hands over his well-muscled chest, feeling his sparse hair against my palms and fingertips. Dragging my hands downward, I feel every ridge of his toned stomach, every mole and scar I've only just started to memorize, until I reach his pants. I make quick work of opening them, and he helps me push them down his hips until they're around his ankles, along with his boxers.

He steps out of them, and I grab a condom and the lube while he lays down on the bed, spread out on his back with his cock laying hard against his stomach, his legs spread just slightly, and a nervous smile on his lips.

I toss the condom and lube down next to him and climb onto the bed, crawling between his legs and pushing them apart as I run my hands up his thighs. His breath hitches, and I consider how long I could spend running my tongue all over his body before he goes insane.

Fuck, I wish I had more than forty-eight hours in Chicago.

I'd be tempted to extend my stay, but we're booked to appear on some daytime talk show on Monday so Lincoln can flash his winning smile and talk about how his struggles are behind him and how happy he is with Jace, and Jude can do his bad boy routine to make the audience swoon before we play one of the new songs Lando wrote.

But all that is Monday Benji's problem. Right now, I have a gorgeous, naked man waiting for me to make him come.

I place a kiss on the center of his chest, and he sighs happily, relaxing into the bed as my mouth makes the same journey my hands did earlier—down his chest, over his stomach, stopping for a short detour to lick the muscles over his hip bone, and ending between his legs. Wrapping my hand around the base of his cock, I pump him slowly, watching as precum beads at his slit. Paris groans.

"Just so I know what *not* to do, can you tell me what made that other time so bad for you?" Most bad bottoming experiences are down to not enough prep or lube, but I don't want to assume.

"He shoved his dick in without lube *or* prep," he says, and I wince. "I told him to stop, and he wouldn't, so I bucked him off and punched him in the face."

I chuckle at that and use my tongue to lap up the precum starting to roll down his shaft.

"Okay, we won't have any problems there then. And if you do need me to stop or slow down, just say so."

"I know; I trust you."

I swallow around a lump in my throat and nod. "How do you feel about rimming?" I ask instead of saying the embarrassingly mushy things I'd like to say.

287

"I've never been rimmed, but I'm up for trying new things," he answers with a smirk.

"Good answer."

I keep stroking him, pushing his legs farther apart before reaching for a pillow to put under is ass to tilt it up so I can get a decent angle.

"This okay on your shoulder?" He hasn't mentioned any issues since he got the sling off, but I notice him wincing from time to time or shifting uncomfortably in certain positions.

"I'm fine," Paris says with a laugh. "Stop checking on me and lick my asshole already."

"God, you're romantic."

I kiss his right ass cheek then the left before parting them and delving into his crease. My tongue finds the rough skin of his pucker, and he squirms, huffing out a little laugh.

"Okay, that's weird," he admits.

"Give it a minute, and if you hate it, I'll stop," I promise.

I tease his entrance with the tip of my tongue, and then full, slow licks with the flat of my tongue, alternating between the two while I wrap my hand around his cock again to stroke him.

"Oh, wow," he breathes, his legs relaxing on either side of me and his cock growing even harder in my hand. I hum triumphantly and lick him deeper, working my tongue inside him until he's flexing his hips and moaning.

Reaching over with my free hand, I grab the lube I set on the bed beside him earlier. I have to stop jerking him off for a second to get my fingers lubed. Replacing my tongue with my fingers, I stroke around his hole while I tongue his balls and return to fisting his erection.

I work one finger inside, taking my time stretching him open.

The sounds filling the room are distant traffic, the blare of the occasional car horn. Much closer: our harsh breathing and the *schick, schick, schick* of my fingers in his ass. Paris' head falls back, and he moans deeply, his toes curling as I hook my finger to hit his sweet spot. It's the most beautiful crescendo.

"Oh fuck, that's good."

I take my time working up to a second finger, and when I ease it inside, Paris tenses for a few seconds before another low moan falls from his lips, music to my ears. I can't take my eyes off his face, the expression of so much pleasure it's nearly painful—his eyebrows scrunched, his jaw slack, a gorgeous blush crawling up his throat into his cheeks.

My heart feels so full for a second I almost can't breathe. It happened so gradually, so naturally that I didn't realize it until this moment; I'm in love with him. Sure, I had a ridiculous crush on Paris when we were teenagers, but what I feel for adult Paris doesn't compare. This is everything—the trust he's putting in me, the way we fit together in every way, the life and future I can't keep myself from imagining with him.

"Please, Benji," Paris begs when I caress his prostate again, this time with two fingers.

"Are you sure you're ready?" I test a third finger, pulling the first two almost all the way out and working a third in beside them. His hole is soft and pliant, his cock standing at attention, hard and leaking, as I fuck him with my fingers.

"I'm ready," he pants.

I slip my fingers out and reach for the condom on the bed, opening it and rolling it on quickly and then adding some more lube before lining up with his hole.

I push his knees up to his chest and hold his gaze, giving him a reassuring smile before I press the head of my cock against his entrance. He hisses, his eyes closing as I push in slowly.

"Doing okay or do you need me to stop?"

"Don't stop."

I lean forward and kiss him, dragging my lips against his in a slow, steady rhythm as I rock my hips gently, filling him inch by inch until I fill him completely.

I kiss him deeper, licking into his mouth as I pull nearly all the way out and hump back into him. Paris' fingers dig into my biceps, our moans mingling to create a harmony of pleasure, the slapping of our skin the percussion. His channel grips my cock, the muscles clenching and fluttering around me with every thrust.

The blush in Paris' cheeks darkens, his breath growing as ragged as mine. I fuck him faster, pushing his knees up higher so I hit his prostate over and over until he's trembling and begging to come.

"You're so sexy, so perfect, I can't believe I get to fuck you," I murmur against his lips as I wrap my hand around his cock and drink in his relieved sob.

"Benji, Benji, ungh," he cries out, his hole squeezing tight around me before starting to pulse, his sticky release spilling over my hand.

I thrust harder, losing my rhythm as my own orgasm overtakes me, starting in the pit of my stomach and washing over me in waves of heat and electricity until I'm completely spent and limp on top of Paris.

"Damn, that was good," Paris says, breathing heavily.

"Mmhmm," I murmur as I nuzzle his throat, using my tongue to lap up droplets of salty sweat.

TRACK 34: SIDE A

I think I love You

Paris

We shower together, unable to keep our hands or lips to ourselves, even after the best sex of my life. Once we get out, we both dress, and Benji takes the time to blow-dry and style his hair and then we snap a picture for social media. Benji tags the venue we're hitting up tonight as well as the band we're going to see. It's not about attention for our relationship anymore; it's about real things like building a name for the record label, bringing attention to the projects we're working on. Maybe it was a silly thing to do at first, to pretend to date, but I can't regret something that gave us a platform to start the early launch for OUTshine or that it brought us together for real.

It's a warm June night as we walk down the street hand in hand, filling each other in on what's been going on since the last time he came to visit in March. We call and text multiple times a day, but there's something different about sharing things in person rather than over the phone. Benji gushes about Archery Records, and we talk more about OUTshine. We had our meeting a few weeks ago, and everything is underway to launch by next year. Our first step is buying properties in New York, LA, and Chicago for the first three centers, and we have someone in charge of scouting places already. It's all falling into place, and even though it's a *huge* project to undertake, we're both over the moon about it.

We take the L and then only have a few more blocks to walk to the bar the band is playing at.

"Tell me about the band we're going to see."

"They're called Electric Blue Stardust. Their demo was fucking awesome, a bit like The Clash but more modern. They're in their early twenties, and they've built quite a name with themselves in the city."

"So, you're going to try to convince them to sign with Archery Records?"

"If they're as good in person as I've heard, I'm sure as hell going to try," he says.

We approach the bar hand in hand, and I notice a few people sneaking pictures of us that I have no doubt will end up online.

Benji has a table reserved. We order a few drinks and enjoy the energy of the bar while we wait for the band to take the stage. I slip my hand under the table to hold Benji's hand again. It's entirely too easy to imagine a life with Benji. Yes, we're both crazy busy, and yes we live in different parts of the country right now, but there's an odd sort of certainty building inside me that this is a whole lot more than just *no longer casual*. But I'm not getting ahead of myself.

The band takes the stage, and Benji's attention becomes laser focused on them. I'm no music expert, but they sound pretty good to me. The lead singer seems to have a lot of energy, and all the songs are pretty catchy; that's about as far as my knowledge goes.

"They're good," I say when there's a break in their playing.

"They're fucking incredible."

"So, you're going to see about signing them?"

"Hell yeah. You want to come with me or wait here?"

"I want to see you in action; let's go."

We slide out of the booth, and I follow Benji as he weaves his way through the crowd toward the backstage area. He hands security a business card and explains why he needs to get backstage, and just like that, they let us through.

We find the band congregating in the green room, talking loudly and sharing a bottle of alcohol.

"Hey, guys," Benji says, knocking at the open door.

The lead singer's eyes go wide as saucers as

he jumps up off the couch.

"Holy fuck, you're Benji Casparian."

"In the flesh."

"I'm Ezra," the front man introduces himself, holding a hand out for Benji to shake. "And this is Nolan, Ayden, and Quinn." He points to each of his bandmates who wave and look various levels of awestruck and shocked. They're so busy fawning over Benji, I might as well be invisible, which works just fine for me.

"What, um...did you watch the set?" Ezra asks, running a hand nervously through his shaggy blond hair.

"We did; you guys fucking rock."

"We do?" Quinn asks, looking around at his bandmates as if he needs to confirm they heard the same thing he just did.

"You seriously do. I actually came out here specifically to see you play," Benji explains, reaching into his pocket and pulling out a business card. "You might've heard that Downward Spiral recently parted ways with Epic Records to form our own recording studio, Archery Records."

Ezra takes the business card from him and stares at it in awe.

"You got ahold of our demo?"

"We did. I think we could make a good team, Electric Blue Stardust and Archery Records. We'd love to fly you guys out to California for an official meeting."

"Is this really happening?" Ayden, the bass player asks.

"It's really happening," Benji confirms with a smile. "Give us a call on Monday if you're interested, and we'll get everything set up for a meeting."

"We absolutely will," Ezra says, practically vibrating with excitement.

After that we leave them to get ready for their next set and head back out to the bar for a few more drinks.

By the time we stumble back into my apartment in the wee hours of the morning, we're both more than a little tipsy and handsy. We make it into my bed at least, rather than humping on the floor like we did back at Benji's place last time I went to visit. And then we get completely lost in each other for a while.

Benji

"Did you see how happy they were when I gave them that business card?" I muse as we lay in bed, naked and sweaty and bathed in moonlight.

"I did," he says, giving me a kiss on the top of the head.

"Downward Spiral has been my heart and soul forever, but there's a different kind of thrill in giving someone else a chance to live this same dream."

"I can see that," Paris says. "Like, you get to

a certain point where you have so much money and stuff, it all becomes meaningless, and you need to find meaning in other places."

"Exactly. It's kind of pathetic really. I thought if I had all this impressive shit and knew all the right people, it would prove that all my success wasn't a mistake. I swear, I woke up every day for ten years expecting someone to come along and tell me I was never meant to have any of this and send me packing back to Ohio to live the tiny, sad life I was really meant for."

"I don't think you're alone. When I got drafted by the Scorpions, it felt like I won the lottery. I was terrified every day I'd lose it all. And then I did, and you know what?"

"What?" I ask, placing a hand over Paris' heart to feel it beat.

"I survived it. I realized, it's not about *belonging* in your life, it's about fighting for the things you want every single day. Downward Spiral survived, but maybe one day you'll decide to break up for good. But that doesn't mean your music is gone. It doesn't mean you won't still have things to give to the world. You don't need anyone else's approval; you are fucking amazing whether you're a fucking rock god or the guy down at the youth center teaching underprivileged kids how to play the piano."

"'Ris?"

"Yeah, Benji?"

"I think I'm in love with you."

A smile spreads over Paris' lips, and I tilt my face up so I can press a kiss to his lips. "I think I'm in love with you, too."

*****

Waking up to the smell of coffee and bacon and the sound of Paris singing to himself in the kitchen is the kind of perfect I couldn't have dreamt up if I tried. I slip out of bed, not bothering with clothes as I head out of the bedroom and toward the kitchen.

"Morning," Paris greets with a smile, standing in the kitchen in nothing but his boxers.

I round the counter and press a kiss to the scar over his right shoulder and then to his lips. "Morning. What's on the agenda for today?"

"I thought we could go for a walk to take a look at a few possible locations for the Chicago home of OUTshine."

"Sounds perfect," I smile. "When do you think you'll be able to make it to New York next? We could do the same out there when you come."

Yes, we have people in charge of this part, but we both agreed we want to be hands on. Plus, it's exciting. We're both like kids on Christmas Eve.

"I'm not sure yet. I meant to tell you yesterday, but I actually have some speaking engagements at a few high school summer sports camps over the next two months. So, I'll probably be pretty busy. You can come out and visit, but I don't think I'll be able to make it to New York again until maybe September?"

"September? That's *ages* away," I complain, instantly feeling bad when Paris looks guilty. "No, it's okay. This is important to you. The last thing I want is this relationship to take away from the other things that are important to us."

I still haven't decided what I'm doing about moving, or if I'll stay in New York. After Paris did his week with *Sports Night,* they offered him a full-time position, but he turned it down. He told me it had nothing to do with whether I'd be living in New York or not, but that he wanted to focus more on his LGBT youth efforts rather than just another way to make money.

"If you're busy, maybe this is a good time for me to get my move done," I muse. "I just can't decide if I want to live in California or if Washington or Oregon would suit me better."

"I've always loved Washington," he offers.

"Yeah? Like, love it enough to want to live there?" I ask, my stomach fluttering nervously as I try to sound casual.

Paris' face remains passive as he pours me a cup of coffee and then plates the eggs and bacon he was cooking and passes it over to me.

"Eventually."

"Eventually," I repeat. "Like...next year?"

Paris sighs. "I don't know, to be honest. I don't want to move too fast."

His brow furrows in worry, and he finally meets my eyes.

"Right, of course," I wave it off like it's no big deal. It's not, but that doesn't stop a gaping hole of disappointment from forming in my chest.

"Benji." He puts a hand under my chin and looks into my eyes. "I'm so in love with you. I'm afraid if we rush into living together, we'll fuck everything up. Going from seeing each other every couple of months to living under the same roof is a *huge* deal. Let's just take things one step at a time, okay?"

I can't argue with his logic so I nod. "You're right."

Paris leans forward and kisses my lips sweetly, and I let out a happy little sigh.

TRACK 35: SIDE A

No Half Measures

Paris

Neither of us bring up the moving in together thing again, but when I drop Benji off at the airport, it feels even harder than usual to part. He clings to me and kisses me over and over but doesn't ask again when we can see each other next. Then, he promises to call me tonight after he's home, and leaves me missing the hell out of him as he walks away.

As soon as I get back to my apartment, I call my brother.

"Hey, how was Benji's visit?"

"Great," I answer with a smile. "Wait, how'd you know he was here?"

"He posted on Instagram about it."

"Oh, right." I get comfortable on the couch and clear my throat as I consider my words. "He wants to move in together."

"That's great."

"Is it?"

"What do you mean? I thought you two were crazy for each other?"

"It's too soon," I answer. "We've only officially been dating two months; we'd be insane to move in together."

I swear I can hear London roll his eyes as he sighs loudly into the phone. "Fine, you've *officially* been dating two months, but you've been falling in love since Christmas. Not to mention your history."

"Being sort-of friends in high school doesn't make it any better," I argue.

"For the love of god, you two were in love with each other back then too."

My face heats. I thought I'd done a good job hiding my feelings for Benji back in high school, but apparently not so much.

"I had a little crush," I correct.

"Yeah, me too," London admits, drawing me up short.

"You had a crush on Benji?"

"Who wouldn't? He's amazing; you know that. Every time we fooled around back then, I hoped he would realize we should be more than friends, but he never had eyes for anyone but you, even when my hand was in his pants." He doesn't sound mad, more resigned than anything, but that doesn't stop guilt from twisting in my gut.

"I'm sorry. I didn't know. You don't still..."

"God, no," he snorts a laugh. "I grew out of that crush as soon as I got to college and realized there were plenty of men in the world other than Benji. But my point is, he's been in love with you all this time. It might seem fast to anyone on the outside, but if you ask me, moving in together is ten years later than it should be."

I roll London's words around in my mind. Is it possible Benji really did have feelings for me back then like he says? Then, the memory of the first time Benji kissed me fills my head, along with Benji and me lying on the floor, sweaty, naked, and covered in cum a few months ago, when he said that he knew it was me when he did it. He didn't just kiss me that night a million years ago, he said he loved me. He told me he loved me, and I thought he meant he loved London, but he didn't.

"I don't think Benji and I should move in together."

"You don't?" he asks, sounding exasperated.

"Nope, I think we should get married."

"Yes!" he agrees enthusiastically. "Wait, is it weird that I've sucked off my future brother-in-law?"

I cringe. "Let's never talk about that, okay?"

"Works for me," he agrees easily. "So, how are you going to propose?"

Benji

I call Archer once I get home and get settled, wanting to tell him right away how it went with Electric Blue Stardust.

"Were they as good in person as the demo made them sound?" Archer asks once we get past greetings and small talk.

"They were incredible. We want this band for Archery Records," I tell him. "They seemed excited about the idea. I think we can definitely sell them on signing with us. The lead singer, Ezra, is going to call to set up a meeting soon. Once he does, I'll fly out for it too."

"Sounds like a plan. Lando and Dawson have been out here this week looking at places," Archer says.

I sigh and lean my head against the back of the couch. "Yeah, I should probably do the same."

"You don't want to leave New York?"

"It's not that. I brought up the idea of moving in together to Paris this weekend, and he wasn't into it. He said it's *too soon*. So, I'm kind of bummed."

"I'm sorry to hear that. I'm sure he'll come around if you give him time."

"Yeah," I agree half-heartedly. I know I'm being impatient. Paris is right; we haven't been officially together all that long. But after six months of only getting to see each other sporadically, I'm more than ready to have him closer.

"Lando says he's got some new songs for you guys, so maybe we can get all the guys together when you come out here and start recording."

"Works for me. I'm more than ready to get back in the studio."

After I hang up with Archer, I'm feeling too antsy to sit at home alone, so I put my shoes back on and decide to go for a walk.

There's something so peaceful to me about getting lost in the bustle of the city. The traffic, so many people walking, all the sounds come together to create a sort of white noise that cocoons me as I walk. Without a destination in mine, I amble down the street for a while, people watching, thinking, trying not to think...

"Hey, Benji." A hand lands on my shoulder, and I turn to see who it is.

"Cooper, what the fuck? You nearly gave me a heart attack," I complain with a laugh.

"Sorry, dude. I was just walking down the street and spotted you. Then I remembered I had like a hundred missed calls from you, and I figured I should catch up with you and see what's up."

I shake my head at him and smile. "Those were from months ago."

"Sorry, I forgot until I saw you."

"It's all good. Are you doing anything right now? Maybe we could go grab a drink and talk?"

"Yeah, let's do it," he agrees, and we beeline for the first bar we spot.

"Word on the street is you guys left Epic. Are you breaking up or what?" Cooper asks once we have drinks in front of us.

"Actually, we're starting our own label."

"No shit?"

"Well, to be more accurate: Archer is starting a label, and we're all investing in it with varying degrees of active roles within it," I explain.

"That's fucking amazing," he says.

"That's actually why I was calling," I hedge.

"What do you mean?" he asks, absently picking at the label on his beer bottle, tearing off little pieces and flicking them away.

"Well, new label, we need talent. I mean, Downward Spiral makes bank, and we're looking at signing an up and coming band, but it's probably best if all of our eggs aren't in one basket. You know of any bands looking for a new label to sign with?" I ask, and Cooper makes an excited sound like I expected.

"Seriously? You're not fucking with me right now?"

"Not at all. If Last Weekend is up for it, we can fly you all out to the current studio in California to show you the recording space and discuss contract terms."

"Let me talk to the guys, but I have a feeling they're going to be all about this. Orion is finally back, and he seems to be doing well.

We've all been itching to make a comeback; we were just hesitant to sign with another big label and end up in the same situation we were in before."

"I can guarantee that won't be the case. Our main focus is artist control. This is *your* music, your art; you should have final say over everything, including your touring and recording schedule."

"It sounds too good to be true," Cooper says with a laugh.

"It's all true," I assure him. "Talk to the guys and let me know."

"I absolutely will."

Cooper and I share a few drinks, shooting the shit and having a few laughs. After we part ways, I give Archer a call to let him know about my talk with Cooper, and he nearly keels over. It feels awesome to be building something like this; it feels like everything I never knew I wanted.

TRACK 36: SIDE A

California

Benji

I get off the plane in California in the middle of August, nearly a month since I last saw Paris in person. Of course, we still video chat, text, and call multiple times a day, but it's not the same. I haven't brought up the idea of living together again, and neither has he. But it's stayed in the back of my mind, constantly there, taunting me with how great it could be...how great it *will* be once Paris is ready.

I grab my suitcase from baggage claim and head outside in search of Jude, who's standing by his car, waiting to take me back to their place.

"Hey," he greets me with a nod, pushing off the car and clapping me on the back.

"Hey, how's it going?"

"It's going," he says with a shrug.

"Staying out of trouble?"

He rolls his eyes at me, but it's not like it used to be; there's no contempt just a resignation to the fact that we're all going to be checking up on him for a while still.

"I'm staying out of trouble."

"Good."

I toss my bag in the backseat and climb into the passenger side, and we pull away.

"You talk to your man recently?" Jude asks once we're on the road driving away from the airport.

I cock my head at the odd question, looking over at him with narrowed eyes. "Yes, why?"

His cheek twitches, and he shrugs. "No reason, just curious."

"Uh-huh," I says suspiciously.

"He couldn't come out this week, right?"

"What's going on? Why are you being weird?"

"I'm not being weird. I'm just taking an interest in your life."

"Riiiiight." I'm not buying that for a second, but I decide to play his game. "I told him we were meeting with a few bands to possibly sign them to the label, and that the official launch party is on Friday, but he's booked solid with speaking engagements and stuff, so he couldn't make it."

"That's a bummer."

"It is," I agree with a hint of annoyance. I know Paris had this stuff all planned long before we set the date for our launch party, but I still wish he could be here for it. "On the bright side, London is flying out for it, so he's going to be my stand-in date."

"Good, good."

"If you're not going to tell me why you're being so weird, can we at least hit a drive-thru for some coffee before we reach the house, because you're giving me a headache."

Jude chuckles and pulls off at the first coffee place we see along the way.

When we get to the house, Lando and Lincoln are already there, along with Lando's boyfriend, Dawson. They're leaving the record label business to Archer and me, but we agreed that this was a great week to start working on the new songs Lando and Lincoln both have for us.

After taking a few minutes to catch up and talk, we head down to the studio in the basement to get a feel for the new songs. I was sent the keyboard parts two weeks ago, so I've been practicing at home and have them all more or less down, but I have no idea how it's going to sound once we all come together. This is always my favorite part, the collaborative feel of making a new song work.

The new music has a bit of a different feel compared to our old stuff. It's still *us*, but...fresh us, if that makes sense. We play until we're all exhausted—arms aching, Lincoln's throat raw, Jude pouring buckets of sweat. But all smiling wider than we have in years.

"This was kick ass," Lincoln declares in a raspy voice. "I need some peppermint tea, stat."

"Yeah, I think it's time for a break," Jude

agrees, and we all abandon our instruments to head upstairs.

We find Archer in the kitchen cooking something that smells amazing.

"How'd it go?" he asks. Jude goes over and gives him a kiss, and Lincoln starts to raid the cupboard for his tea, while Lando and I both take a seat at the kitchen table.

"It went amazing. I think we'll be able to start recording tomorrow after we wrap up our meetings with EBS and Last Weekend," I say.

"As long as I rest my voice tonight," Lincoln agrees.

"Great. I'm excited to work on the marketing plan the new PR firm gave us for this one."

"Me too," I agree.

Paris

Sitting in the bustling airport, waiting for my plane to board, I run my finger along the small, velvet ring box in my pocket, and think about Benji. London and I brainstormed a million ideas of times and places for me to propose; I just hope Benji is happy with what I came up with.

My phone vibrates in my other pocket, and I pull it out to see a text from my brother along with an attached video clip.

London: Your man is a sloppy drunk

The video is of Benji and the rest of the band around a bonfire. There are about eight other guys as well, I recognize them from Electric Blue Stardust and Last Weekend. Benji sways with a drink in his hand, singing off key as Lincoln strums a guitar and they all laugh.

"*I feel very secure in my position as lead singer,*" he jokes.

"*Don't hate me 'cause you ain't me,*" Benji quips back with a smug smile, and the video ends.

I smile and put my phone back down, a longing ache starting in my chest. Soon we won't have to wait weeks or months between seeing each other. Soon, we'll call the same place home. It doesn't matter where he decides he wants to live. Wherever he is, that's where I want to be. Wherever he is, that's where home is.

"Um, excuse me," a timid voice says.

I put my phone away and look up to see a young man, probably in his late teens, wearing an Arizona football jersey and shuffling his feet nervously.

"Hi," I say.

"Sorry to bother you. I was debating with myself for like twenty minutes if I should come over here or not."

"It's no bother, just waiting on my plane," I assure him.

"I wanted to tell you what an inspiration

you are." He swallows hard, his Adam's apple bobbing and a blush painting his cheeks. "I was about to start my freshman year of high school when you came out, and I didn't plan on trying out for the football team because I'm gay. But then you came out, and I thought, if a pro player can be gay, then maybe it's okay. It changed my life. I took my boyfriend to prom and was prom king, and in the fall I have a scholarship to ASU to play linebacker." He plucks at his jersey for emphasis. "So, I owe you a big thank you. Without football, I wouldn't be able to afford college, and without you, I wouldn't have had the guts to go out for the team. You're my hero."

Emotion swells in my throat. "I wasn't trying to be a hero, but I'm glad I inspired you to live your best life." I know it sounds a little corny, but I mean every word.

"Anyway, thanks again. And I hope you and Benji are really happy together. You guys are total hashtag relationship goals."

I chuckle, making a mental note to tell Benji. He'll get a kick out of it.

"Thank you. Just between you and me, I'm going to propose this weekend. Wish me luck."

He lights up with a smile. "Good luck."

The boarding call for my flight is announced so I stand and hold my hand out for him, pulling him in to clap him on the back.

"Good luck with everything, I'll be watching for you in the draft in a few years." I give him an encouraging smile and get on the plane to go claim the rest of my life.

TRACK 37: SIDE A

The Rest of Our Lives

Benji

"Are you *sure* you can't make it out here for the launch party tonight?" I pout on the phone to Paris while I lay in bed in one of Archer's many guest bedrooms.

"I wish I could," Paris says with a sigh. "I'm in New Jersey."

"This sucks. If I was home in New York I could see you."

"I know, it does suck, but we'll get it figured out soon," he assures me.

"Yeah," I sigh, unconvinced. The only way I can see fixing the problem of not being able to see each other often enough would be to move in together, but I'm not about to bring that up again.

"What are you wearing to the party?" he asks, deftly changing the subject.

"Clothes," I answer petulantly.

"Too bad," he chuckles.

"I want you here."

"And I want to be there."

"I know you do. I'm sorry; I just miss the hell out of you," I apologize. This is exactly why I knew a relationship was a bad idea to begin with, but it was impossible not to fall in love with Paris. And as much as it sucks that we're both so busy, it's worth it to have him. "I love you."

"I love you, too. More than anything," he says.

"I guess I'll let you go so I can get up and shower. I need to make sure everything's ready for tonight, and my to-do list is about a mile long."

"It's going to go off without a hitch, and you're going to call me and tell me how amazing it was first thing tomorrow morning."

"Yes, I will. But first I'm going to spend the day texting you everything that goes wrong so you can be miserable with me."

"Deal," Paris agrees. "I'll talk to you later."

"Later."

I lay in bed a few minutes longer before managing to drag my ass to the shower, a mental checklist for the day forming as I wash up and then get out and blow-dry my hair.

There's a tap at my door, and London peeks his head in.

"Hey, wasn't sure if you were up yet," he says.

"I'm up, showered, and just about ready to go," I assure him, pulling my shirt over my head and then running a brush through my hair one last time. "Thanks for being here to help me with everything today and being my date tonight."

"When have I ever turned down the chance for a date with Benji Casparian?" he jokes.

Things go smoother than I expected with only a few minor snags throughout the day as the party draws near. About an hour before the event, London and I head back to the house to get dressed.

"Don't wear that; wear your blue suit," he says when he sees me pulling out my charcoal gray suit.

"This is a nice suit," I argue.

"But the blue one makes your eyes pop. You look great in it."

"Since when are you a fashion guru? You're my date for the night, and all the sudden I'm a woman from the nineteen fifties who needs to be told how to dress?"

"Fine, wear what you want, but don't come crying to me later."

"Later when? Why is everyone being so weird this week?" I grumble, putting the gray suit back into the closet and grabbing the blue one.

"Hey, Benji?" London says, sounding suddenly serious.

"Yeah?"

"You're my best friend, and I love you."

"I love you too, but you're freaking me out. Are you dying or something?" I dart my eyes over him, searching for some external cause of my best friend's behavior.

"I'm not dying," he assures me. "I'm going to get dressed so I won't hold anyone up."

"Okay, weirdo."

He disappears, and I get dressed and fix my hair. We meet up with the rest of the guys in the living room a few minutes later, all of them dressed to the nines. Our limo is waiting outside to take us to the venue for the party.

The guest list for the launch party is impressive, with industry people, artists, and a number of other celebrities. It's going to be huge. We're planning to announce tonight that Last Weekend and Electric Blue Stardust are signed with Archery Records as well, and basically spend the night rubbing elbows and looking impressive.

Epic Records even sent a congratulatory bottle of champagne to Archer last night, which we all broke open and shared on the back deck while shit talking Epic and plotting ways to steal more bands from them—all in good fun, of course.

We all pile into the limo outside, and Lincoln opens a bottle of whiskey from the minibar, pouring it into glasses for each of us, except Jude who gets water instead, and passing them out.

"We've all come a long way in the past ten

years, but without Archer, we wouldn't be here. He made our dreams come true, and it's an absolute honor to do the same for him," Lincoln toasts.

"Here, here," I say, raising my class, and all the other guys do the same.

"I'm prouder than hell, Archie; you're amazing," Bennett says, giving Archer a kiss.

"I can't thank you all enough," Archer says, clinking his glass to each of ours. "Especially you, Benji. You signed two incredible bands, helped me make all the decisions, and took this entire party onto your shoulders."

"My pleasure, Arch." I tap his glass with mine, and we both take a drink.

The limo pulls up to the venue, and I reach for London's hand. "You ready to face your first barrage of press?"

"As ready as I'll ever be," he says, squeezing my hand and climbing out of the limo with me.

Cameras flash as we make our way into the building. We wave and smile, answering as many questions as we can on our way inside. It amuses me to wonder what they'll make of me with London instead of Paris. I'm sure it'll be funny to see the spin they put on it.

Once we're inside, the first order of business is drinks, and then we all start making our rounds, talking to all manner of rich and self-important people.

London seems distracted as we mingle,

constantly looking around like he's trying to spot someone. But every time I ask him, he waves me off. He checks his phone more than once, and I'm about to snatch it out of his hand and keep it for the night so he can focus on enjoying the party when his eyes light up as he looks at something, or someone, over my shoulder.

I turn to see what has him so excited, and my breath catches.

Paris

The look on Benji's face when he realizes I'm here is priceless and completely worth the lie about not being able to make it tonight.

"Oh my god, you're here."

"I'm here," I confirm with a chuckle, opening my arms and bracing as he flings himself at me, careful as always to keep the impact to my left side.

"What are you doing here? Were you lying this morning?"

"I was lying. Are you mad?"

"You're here; how could I be mad? But why'd you lie?"

"I thought the surprise would be more fun."

"Surprises are fun," Benji agrees, nuzzling against my neck and squeezing his arms around my waist.

"I've been thinking about what you mentioned last time you were in Chicago."

He stills in my arms, drawing back to look up at me with cautious hope in his eyes. "About what exactly?"

"About moving in together."

"And what do you think about it?"

I reach into my pocket, dragging my finger along the velvet outside of the ring box. Taking a deep breath to steady my nerves, I pull it out. Everyone around us grows quiet as I drop to one knee, and Benji's eyes go wide. In my peripheral vision, I can see his bandmates gathered around, and London off to my left filming the whole thing with his phone.

"I think you're the love of my life. I think I fell in love with you when I was thirteen without realizing it, and from that moment on, no one else has ever been good enough. I think I want to spend the rest of my life with you."

"Oh my god," Benji says, putting his hands in front of his mouth as a tear runs down his cheek. "Is this real?"

"It's real. Say yes?"

"You didn't officially ask," he points out.

"Oh shoot, you interrupted me and threw me off," I complain, and we both laugh. "Benjamin Clark Casparian, will you marry me?"

"Hell yes, I will." He holds his hand out eagerly, and I take the ring out of the box and slip it onto his finger and then kiss the back of his hand.

I stand up, and Benji's in my arms again

in an instant, peppering kisses all over my face while everyone cheers.

"Think anyone will notice if we find a coat closet to hook up in, because getting engaged made me horny as fuck," he whispers into my ear, his breath hot against my neck, his body flush against mine so I can feel the truth of his words as it presses against me.

"Let's go," I agree, dragging him out of the main hall in search of somewhere we can fool around.

We end up in a utility closet with the door locked, fumbling with each other's pants as we share hungry kisses. Murmuring *I love you* to each other over and over. For so long I thought my injury was the worst thing that ever happened to me, but I think that was because I couldn't see where the path was leading until now. If I hadn't been injured, Elliot and I might not have broken up when we did. I wouldn't have Benji. I wouldn't have OUTshine. I wouldn't have this amazing, meaningful life with the most incredible man I've ever met.

Benji gets my pants down and drops to his knees in front of me, taking my cock into his mouth eagerly.

"Fuck," I mutter, threading my fingers through his hair as he sucks me long and deep, hollowing his cheeks and making obscene slurping sounds that settle in my balls and drive me wild. He looks up at me through his eyelashes, his lips stretched wide around my cock, and it hits me like a ton of bricks that this man is going to be my husband. I couldn't have held back my orgasm if I'd tried.

Benji moans as my cock throbs in his mouth, my release painting his tongue and hitting the back of his throat. My hips twitch, and I groan as I empty myself down his throat.

"Can we put a promise of blowjobs into our wedding vows?" I ask as he licks the remnants of cum from my over-sensitive cock before tucking it back into my pants.

"You'd better believe that'll be in my vows."

"God, I fucking love you."

"I fucking love you too."

EPILOGUE

Benji

Cheers from the crowd accompany the steady rhythm of the song Electric Blue Stardust is rocking out. I pull back the curtain a fraction to see them in action. They're owning the stage like they were born to be there. Ezra rivals Lincoln in stage presence, and the rest of the guys don't shy away from living up to the example he sets. They're going to be stars; I'm sure of it.

"They remind me of us ten years ago," Lincoln muses, coming up behind me.

"We wish," I snort. "They have their shit way more together than we did on our tour with Last Weekend."

"Don't jinx them," Lando scolds, joining our little group.

I turn my attention back to the band on stage for a few more minutes. It's an amazing feeling to know I had a hand in picking them out of thousands and putting them on one of the biggest stages in the world, opening for our first tour since leaving Epic Records just over a year ago. This is the start of a whole new chapter for the band, and for all of us, and it fills me up inside to know I gave them a new start too.

I look out into the crowd and see Jace, Lincoln's husband, in the front row beside Paris and Dawson. Lincoln and Jace got married six months ago in a small ceremony only the band and Jace's brother were invited too. I've never seen two people happier than they were on their wedding day.

We told our men they didn't have to watch from the crowd, that they could enjoy the whole concert from backstage, but they all insisted they wanted the full experience. I glance over at Lincoln to find him smiling widely, his entire face lit up with pure joy as he stares unashamed at his husband. Lando isn't much better, making googly eyes at Dawson from afar.

After the studio and the rest of the band relocated to the West coast, Lando and Dawson followed suit, getting a small house in Washington state. Not that they spend much time there, choosing instead to keep busy with all kinds of travel and adventures. Dawson finished writing a book that he's been shopping around to publishers as well, and from what I hear, Lando is planning to propose soon as well.

It's hard to believe how far we've all come in the past year, and how much happiness we all have now. As hard earned as it was, I don't think any of us would say it wasn't worth it.

Thanks to a suggestion from Dawson, we've made the tour deaf friendly by having the lyrics to the songs appear on a huge screen behind us for each song, and we hired a lighting artist to create a light show that pulses with the beat of each song.

"We've come a long way."

"And the road was rough as fuck," Lincoln adds with a wry smile. "I've got the scars to prove it."

I put an arm around my friend and give him a hug.

"I have a good feeling things are going to start looking up from here."

"Me too."

"What'd I miss?" Jude asks, finally joining us as well, looking a little disheveled.

"Busy getting a little before the show quickie?" I tease, and he blushes a little.

"I was...um...this is hard."

"You don't have to tell us if you don't want to," Lincoln assures him.

"No, I mean, *this* is hard. Being sober at the house in California, it's like, my brain knows it's different so it's not as hard. But being backstage, all the sights and sounds of tour fucking with my head," he explains, shaking his head at himself. "Bennett could tell I was struggling, so he took me to the bus and spanked me to help center me, help me focus my mind more."

"Whatever you have to do to stay sober," Lando says, patting Jude on the shoulder.

Jude nods and gives us all a grateful look.

Electric Blue Stardust wraps up the last song of their set and, after the stage crew quickly switches out their instruments for ours, it's our turn to take the stage.

The cheers are deafening as we get into our places, and Lincoln takes the microphone.

"What's up, New York?" he asks, receiving a deafening roar in response. "We're so glad to be here tonight. I know we've been good at keeping it under wraps, but the band went through a rough time last year," he says to a round of laughter. "It was love from you guys that kept us going, and for that, we owe you a huge debt of gratitude. Now, how about we play some fucking music?" Another cheer and Jude taps out a countdown to launch us into our first song.

Paris

Watching Benji on stage is like a religious experience. I've watched him play a hundred times, but it never ceases to leave me with my jaw on the floor. He looks like a god, beautiful and fierce, becoming one with the music as it flows through him. Somehow, I find a way to fall in love with him even more in this moment, and it takes my breath away.

Beside me, Dawson, Jace, Bennett, and Archer—who just joined us—seem to be experiencing the same feelings for their men up on that stage. When Benji first invited me to come on tour with them, I balked a little at the idea of feeling like a groupie, but I'm glad I got over that and got the chance to experience this with him.

The tour is short, only spanning the next eight weeks, ending in Florida where Benji and I will be flying our families in for our beach wedding. We're keeping it completely under wraps from anyone but the band and our families, so the press won't catch wind of it. We'll do a press release after, but the wedding itself is just for us.

We're both still keeping more than busy, always finding new causes, new projects, new paths to explore. But now we come home to each other at the end of every day, and sometimes we chase our new paths together. Our lives may be hectic, but to us, they're absolutely perfect.

Benji glances over at me, shooting me a little wink that makes my heart flutter. I wouldn't change a single thing about our crazy, beautiful lives for anything in the world.

**

Thank you for enjoying the Replay series! If you enjoyed a bit of angst the K.M. Neuhold way, you'll LOVE my stand alone Change of Heart. Can love live on even after a heart transplant? Grab it now

ABOUT THE AUTHOR

K.M. Neuhold is a complete romance junkie. Pansexual and polyamorous, she often describes herself as being in love with love. She loves to write stories full of bearded, cinnamon roll men who get super swoony HEAs. Her philosophy is there's so much angst and sadness for LGBT characters in media, all she wants is to give them the happiest happily ever afters she can with little angst, tons of humor, and SO MUCH STEAM. K.M. fully admits to her tendencies of making sure every side character has a full backstory that will likely always lead to every book turning into a series or spin-off. When she's not writing she's a lion tamer, an astronaut, and a superhero...just kidding, she's likely watching Netflix and snuggling with her husky while her amazing husband brings her coffee.

Made in the USA
Middletown, DE
03 October 2023